D1315005

After Aesop:
Stories for All Ages

Aaron McEmrys
Illustrations by **Lisa Hedicker**

ROSE · WINDOW · MEDIA
rosewindowmedia.com

Rose Window Media
1535 Santa Barbara Street
Santa Barbara, California 93101

First Edition, 2011

rosewindowmedia.com

Printed in the United States of America

Book design by Alex Abatie

—For my children Alex, Zoe, Nathan, and Luke

*No act of kindness, no matter how small,
is ever wasted. —Aesop*

Table of Contents

Foreword   15

How to Use This Book   19

About the Icons   22

The Stories

The Lion Who Always Said "I'm Sorry" . . .   25

The Fort   32

Permits, Please   40

How Raven Freed the Sun   46

Squirrels Vs. Blue Jays   53

Tippy the Cat 58

The Case of the Stolen Cookies 63

A Town Called Driftwood 69

The President Who Got Fed Up 75

The (H)Edge of the World 83

The Stolen Hearts 90

Earth at the Interplanetary Conference 97

The Bagheads 103

Be Careful What You Wish For:
A Halloween Story 107

Brave Raven 114

You Can't Stop the Music 119

Winter Solstice: The Bottom of the Well . . 125

The End of Beavertown 136

The Story of Dog and Duck 142

The Rainbow Bridge 149

Bee Strike 156

Summer Camp Blues 164

Mirror, Mirror 170

The Emperor Who Was Afraid
of Bunny Rabbits 176

The Broken Flute 183

A Church Mouse Christmas 188

Robots in Love 194

The Medicine Tree 201

The Seagull and the Garbage Dump 209

The Wonders of Duct Tape 215

Too Much of a Good Thing 220

The Field: An Easter Story 226

The Perfect Party 232

We Are Not Afraid 241

Acknowledgements 247

Foreword

Most children's books these days are bound in paper and transient in nature, but this book by Aaron McEmrys stands apart. In both content and form, this volume is substantial, strong and sturdy. The book itself and the stories it contains are designed to be held in many hands, read and reread, and then to be passed along to new generations. This is a generous keepsake of a book—a great gift from a gifted minister.

Inspired by Aesop, Sufi tales, and midrash from scripture, Aaron has taken his model for *After Aesop: Stories for All Ages* from ageless tales. The best of his stories have the heft and resonance of these classics—but they are not in the least bit stuffy. These stories are full of humor and satire, and many are touched with the irony characteristic of ancient morality tales. The themes are universal: "How Raven Freed the Sun" encourages readers to own their own strength; "Can't Stop the Music" tells of the irrepressible life force that lives within us, urging us on even in difficult times; "The Medicine Tree" illustrates the nature of greed and the grace of forgiveness.

This volume is meant to be shared. I can envision a father holding the book on a sofa, with a four-year-old on one side and a ten-year old on the other, all three experiencing a story about that legendary trickster, Raven, at different levels. The four-year-old laughs at the silliness of the animal characters and wonders what will happen during the scary parts. The ten-year-old picks up on the plot, but also catches the many pop-culture allusions. The father is moved because even as a mature adult, he still harbors fears of showing his moral strength, as Raven learns to do.

Aaron's sense of language and voice are as sturdy and trustworthy as the bound volume itself. His unique combination of his naturally prophetic voice with funky animal and robot fables yields stories that are at once funny and wistful. Reading the stories, one experiences this writer/preacher as a person of integrity, a person who possesses an abundance of what we used to call "character." Although he is charming, wise, and gentle, never taking himself too seriously, Aaron's fierce sense of justice and his acceptance of the reality of evil in the world shine through here, as do the ancient stories that inspired him.

I would be amiss if I did not call attention to Lisa Hedicker's fine illustrations, which fully match Aaron's humor, depth, and sensitivity. These are pictures created with obvious love and purpose, in exquisite detail and arresting color. Readers will want to look and look, and look again.

Aaron wrote these stories while carrying on a full-time ministry— an amazing feat in its own right. He wanted the children of the congregation to know that he was their minister, too, and that each week he spent special time preparing for them, as well as for the adults. How fortunate for the rest of us! We have reaped the benefits of his caring.

—Marilyn Sewell

Reverend Dr. Marilyn Sewell is Minister Emerita of the First Unitarian Church, Portland, Oregon. She served as the church's Senior Minister for 17 years. A well-known writer, activist, and spiritual leader, Marilyn was featured in Peter Wiedensmith's documentary "Raw Faith," which was released in April of 2010.

How to Use This Book

WHEN I WAS A little boy, my sisters and I loved to sit on Grandma Arlene's lap for a bedtime story. How she fit all three of us on her lap at one time is still a mystery to me today, but we all loved to hear her read from old, battered copies of Thorton Burgess's *Old Mother West Wind* stories. They were our favorites.

Although the pages were worn and yellow-brown with age, Burgess' tales were very much alive. They touched something in my sisters and I that other stories didn't. They weren't just entertaining—they were challenging! So were the discussions they inspired in those precious minutes before bed: *What does it mean to be a good person? To be part of a family? A community? A world?* These were the first moral conversations of my life, and they stuck with me.

Years later, in my early twenties, I found myself thumbing through old spines in a little charity bookstore in Cooperstown, New York. On an impulse, I asked the elderly woman behind the counter if she had any books by Thorton Burgess. "My grandmother used to read them to me," I told her.

Her eyes lit up. "Why, Thornton Burgess! Really. When I was a child, my father used to read his stories to us out of the paper every Sunday! We'd pile up on his lap on the porch swing…" she went on, and I watched her eyes grow distant with memory.

As we reminisced together about how much those stories meant to us, an identical light shone through our eyes. I could see the little girl she had been 75 years before, sitting on her father's knee to hear stories—the kind of stories meant to be shared, reflected upon and returned to by people of all ages.

In that moment, I realized I wanted to create stories in the same tradition. Now, I do, as a father and as a part of my work as a Unitarian Universalist minister. I write a new story almost every week for the children of all ages in my congregation. I write these stories not just for the literal children sitting at my feet, but also for the children who still live inside every grownup. These are the stories gathered between the covers of this, my first book of Stories for All Ages.

The stories in this book explore universal issues and timeless human themes like empowerment, freedom, responsibility, compassion, justice and sacrifice, with an intent to foster the asking of life's big questions—to inspire spirited, wonder-filled discussion and curiosity.

These are not just Unitarian Universalist stories. They are teaching stories written in the tradition of Aesop's fables, Jewish midrash and Sufi teaching stories. They are stories employed as vehicles for wisdom. A teaching story is meant to entertain, but it is also meant to inspire insight and learning. Teaching stories aren't just for children, but for an intergenerational community—a jumping-off point for conversation between adults and children.

In the modern world, adults and children have few venues in which to talk about life's big questions. Most of the stories found in bookstores these days are age-stratified: there are books for children and books for grownups. And this is a shame, because most of us wrestle with life's big questions throughout life—not just in childhood. A good conversation about fairness, forgiveness, inclusivity or gratitude, serves everyone who shows up for it. Often, the kids have just as much wisdom to share as the adults do when those conversations happen!

My hope is that these stories will particularly help to foster conversation about freedom, on which our culture places very high value; and its oft-forgotten balancing factor, responsibility. We want to be free to be who we really are and to do the things that are important to us; the big question here is: what responsibilities come with that freedom? How should we fulfill them? How can we support others in striking that balance between freedom and responsibility? Many of these stories touch upon this balance. I encourage families and communities to read and discuss them with this in mind.

Sharing stories is fundamentally different from reading them alone. Like other teaching stories, these are designed to be shared. Individuals can enjoy and find value here, but I encourage the reading of these stories in the context of families and communities—places where the act of sharing is every bit as important as the content of the stories themselves. To this day, when I think of Burgess' stories, I still hear them in my grandmother's voice. These are precious memories for me, and I hope you will use the stories in these pages to create similar memories with young people in your life.

About the Icons

THIS BOOK IS DESIGNED to explore specific themes as they come up in the lives of children of all ages. My hope is that you'll use these tales as conversation starters and ways to create connectedness between children and adults around asking and talking about life's big questions. To make this easier, we've developed a "map" that can be used to identify stories most relevant to whatever situations children in your life might be facing.

At the beginning of each story, you'll see this list of icons in the top right-hand corner of the right-hand page. The icons that are highlighted convey the themes of that story. (Most of the stories address several themes, as any good story should.) At the end of each story, you'll find at least one discussion question to help adults and children talk about how the story's themes are reflected in their own lives.

 MAKING A DIFFERENCE Children naturally want to help make the world a better place. These stories help children reflect upon ways in which they can help and serve others.

 COMING TOGETHER These stories are about learning to accept, like, and even love one another despite differences.

 FORGIVING This is one of the hardest things we do in our lives and one of the most valuable. These stories are about forgiving others and about asking for and accepting forgiveness when we need it ourselves.

HOLIDAY TALES These tales are meant to foster a deeper understanding of the true meaning of the holidays we celebrate.

 TAKING A JOURNEY The full life is full of many kinds of journeys: through space, through time, and through rites of passage. Courage is often required by those who begin and complete big journeys. These stories encourage readers to consider and celebrate the journeys they've taken and those that still lie ahead.

 SECOND CHANCES We all make mistakes. No one likes having done so, but as most adults know making mistakes is a very important way we learn. These stories are about people and other creatures who mess up and are then presented with a second chance to get it right.

 EARTH How can we help save the natural world from damage done by our fellow human beings? How can we have a less detrimental impact on the Earth in our own lives? These stories encourage children of all ages to reflect upon the beauty of this planet and what they can do to ensure that it can be enjoyed and appreciated by many, many more generations.

 BEING YOURSELF These are stories about people, animals and other kinds of creatures (think robots!) who are untrue to themselves, but then find a way to discover and embrace who they really are.

 GIVING In our consumerist society, it can be hard for children of any age (including those old enough to be called "grownups") to remember that giving is as rewarding as receiving; sometimes, it's even more so. Stories with this icon provide gentle reminders of the value of giving to others, and not just presents: we can give abundant time, love, and support.

The Lion Who Always Said "I'm Sorry"

ONCE UPON A TIME, there was a lion who was friendly and well-groomed. He always kept his claws, paws, teeth and coat immaculately clean and tidy. When he walked by, his glossy coat shimmering in the bright sun, all of his mother's friends would say, "What a very well-groomed young lion he is!" His name was Sekhar (pronounced, "shaker").

But above all, Sekhar was polite. His mother and father had taught him from his earliest cub-hood that "good manners make the lion" and "courtesy is the backbone of civilization." It would be very hard indeed to find another lion anywhere who was as polite as this one.

The lion spent a lot of time hunting, as lions are wont to do. No matter how many herbivores he devoured, he was always very hungry, But no matter how much Sekhar's tummy rumbled or how impatiently he wanted to pop another little critter in his mouth, he never forgot his manners.

"Excuse me," he said, as he pinned some scared creature beneath his powerful paws, "I'm terribly sorry, but I'm afraid I am going to eat you now. Really, I'm most terribly sorry." And even after he had popped his unfortunate lunch into his terrible jaws, Sekhar kept apologizing. "Terribly sorry, old chap ... so sorry ... you're very tasty, did you know that? Do please accept my humble apology." When the last morsel was swallowed, he let out a satisfied burp—which he always covered politely with his paw, just as he had been taught to do.

This drove the prey animals of the savannah crazy! It was bad enough that he went around eating them all the time, but the constant apologizing was too much. Finally, after much discussion, they decided to teach Sekhar a lesson.

The animals went to a special pool in the deepest part of the jungle. There, in an old and mighty tree, lived a

magic bird named Hoopoe. Hoopoe, who could shape-shift whenever she liked, listened carefully to the animals' complaints. After much reflection, she agreed to help them.

The bird flew like the wind to Sekhar's favorite hunting grounds and waited for him on the branch of a small tree. On that day, Hoopoe was a tiny bird, barely a mouthful for a lion. But her feathers were bright and beautiful, and her eyes shone like jewels. She knew the lion would never be able to resist such a scrumptious appetizer.

In due time, the young lion crept up behind Hoopoe,

slowly rising up behind her, readying his sharp claws and glistening fangs. He was falling right into her trap. With lightning speed, Sekhar caught Hoopoe in his claws. Then he said, "Oh, beautiful bird, jewel of the savannah, I am very sorry and I must apologize most profusely in advance, for I am about to eat you. *Terribly* sorry."

"Oh, lion," she said, "you are a lion, and lions must hunt. All the animals of the forest understand that. But I can see in your eyes that there is no sorrow in you. Your apologies are hollow. Beware, for there is nothing in this world so sure to leave you sad and alone as false tears."

The lion considered the little bird for a moment. Then he smiled and said, "Thanks for the advice, little gem, but you are not my teacher, only my snack! Terribly, terribly sorry!" And with that, Sekhar popped her into his mouth and swallowed her in one gulp. He licked his chops and felt very satisfied with himself.

Remember, Hoopoe was just a tiny thing, just enough of a morsel to make the lion feel even hungrier. So he got into his best hunting crouch and stalked off across the meadows in search of an entrée. That's when things started to go terribly wrong for the exceedingly polite, extremely well-groomed young lion.

Every time he got anywhere near water holes where

succulent water buffalo were drinking, and every time he crept close to a tasty family of Thompson's gazelles or a nice swamp-marinated hippo, the little bird in his belly began to sing.

Loud and clear and crystalline, Hoopoe's song rose up from deep inside him, forcing its way through his clenched fangs. "Danger," she sang, "danger, here comes an untrustworthy lion!" And the animals, duly warned, scattered before Sekhar could get close enough to pounce.

After a few days of this the lion was absolutely famished. Every time he tried to get close to his prey, the magic Hoopoe starting singing and the animals escaped. For the first time in his life, he was afraid he might starve to death. Terrified, hungry and desperate, the lion roamed across the savannah begging for help, the Hoopoe's song still filling the air. But the other animals did not trust him and would not answer his call.

Finally, Sekhar just lay down next to the big watering hole to die. He felt stark terror and grief at the thought that he would never see his parents again, never walk proud under the bright blue sky again. In those moments of being so afraid and lonesome, he realized in a flash that this was probably exactly what all the little animals felt just before he ate them. How coldly proper and polite he had been—and what a fool! Sekhar felt sorry and ashamed.

Many other animals had gathered around. "I have
been so wrong, my friends, thinking only of myself," he
told them. "I am a lion, and so I must eat you to live, but
I should have respected you enough to do so with honor.
Instead, I mocked you with false apologies and made you
hate me." With that, a few tears of genuine sorrow began
to run down the lion's face. "I am so sorry. Please…forgive
me before I die." He was truly sorry!

Suddenly, he felt something moving in his tummy.
With the most impolite burp, Sekhar opened his mouth,
and the magic bird flew out and lit upon a nearby tree.

The animals forgave the lion. Not for eating them,
which they knew lions just had to do. No, they forgave him
for his irritating, relentless, dishonest apologies.

To this once fierce lion, now so weak he could barely
move, the animals brought delicious bowls of hummus
and falafel and lots of other vegetarian delights. Sekhar
was surprised at how tasty everything was and before long,
he had lost interest in hunting altogether. The gazelles
and zebras and meerkats taught him all their secret
recipes. Soon, Sekhar had become a very accomplished
vegetarian chef. He let his mane grow into a wild tangle
of dreadlocks, started wearing Birkenstock sandals and

moved to Portland, Oregon to open a hip vegan café
called Wildwood. And there he lives, to this very day.

DISCUSSION QUESTION:
*If you think you've done something that hurt someone else, what could
you do instead of saying you're sorry?*

The Fort

JOSIE LOVED FORTS. She was adept at building several different kinds of forts, some of the indoor variety and some of the outdoor variety. But her favorite fort of all was the Classic Blanket Fort.

She'd take all the chairs from the dining room table and make a circle out of them on the thick living room carpet. Then, she stripped all the blankets and colorful quilts from her bed and draped them over the high chair backs until all the open space was covered up—except for a tiny door for crawling through. And she always left a couple of spy holes in her blanket forts so that she could keep a sharp lookout for Jeb, her little brother.

Oh but she couldn't *stand* that pest Jeb. He was always following her around and bugging her. The one place he was never allowed was inside her forts. *No boys allowed.* That was her rule.

It was cool and dim inside the blanket fort. The light from the living room windows filtered through the fabric of her bright quilt in a patchwork of colors, like stained glass. She felt safe and snug inside.

One snowy winter day, Josie was headed outside for a big neighborhood snowball fight when Jeb raced down the stairs after her, bundled from head to toe in winter clothes. "Wait for me!" he cried. "Mom says you have to take me with you!"

Josie yelled back, "No way! You always cry. Every single time."

"*Mom says,*" Jeb replied darkly, and Josie knew she was stuck with him.

Across the street they went to the big lawn by the apartment buildings, where all the best snow fights happened. There must have been twenty kids there. Snowballs whizzed through the air, plopped wetly onto the ploughed street and into trees, and splattered against nylon winter jackets. It was awesome … for about three minutes, anyway.

At right about that three-minute mark, Josie aimed a big wet snowball at Thomas, a kid from her class. Thomas ducked and the snowball went over his head—and hit her little brother square in the face.

Jeb staggered toward her, his face covered with a mush of cold snow. He was crying in that way where no sound comes out. There's just a wide-open mouth, squinched-shut eyes and plenty of tears. As she cleared the snow from Jeb's face, she saw that his nose and cheeks were bright, scarlet red. Josie had a sinking feeling in her stomach.

As soon as Jeb could stop crying long enough to speak, he yelled, *"I'm telling Mom!"* And he took off running back to their house.

Josie ran after him. "I'm sorry! Jeb, *seriously*! It was an accident! *Don't tell Mom!*" But Jeb didn't listen. Off he sloshed, and Josie knew she was in trouble. Within a minute, she heard her mother's strident voice calling her in from the best snow fight of the whole winter.

Josie tried and tried to explain that she hadn't whomped her brother in the face with a snowball on purpose. Her mom just shook her head and said, "Josie, Jeb is your brother and you have to watch out for him, no matter what." She was sent to bed early that night. And it wasn't fair at all.

The next morning was Saturday. Josie got up, went downstairs and built the biggest, best blanket fort ever. It filled up almost the whole living room. Josie loaded up the fort with all her favorite things: her books, markers, favorite stuffed animals and a couple of boxes of graham crackers. Then she went into the kitchen and made a very important announcement.

"Mother and Jeb," she said firmly, "I hereby declare my fort an independent country. I am the President. No one but me is allowed in, no matter what. I have everything I need, and I will not live for one more minute in this terrible kingdom."

She then spun on her heels, her dignified nose in the air. Into her fort she crawled, never to come out again.

Josie had fun in there for a while. She smiled to herself, thinking how much everyone would miss her now that she had seceded from the family. Being the queen of her own kingdom felt pretty good.

But then, it started to get a little stuffy in there, with all those thick blankets piled above like a roof. And the graham crackers were tasty, but when she realized that she had forgotten to stock her fort with milk, she had to sneak quietly onto foreign soil to liberate some. And of course, when nature called, she had to tiptoe over to the bathroom that adjoined the living room.

Hours passed, and Josie started to worry that her hamster, Napoleon, might be lonely without her. So she snuck upstairs to fetch him, big glass cage and all.

Still more time passed. She had already thumbed through all of her books, and it wasn't even nighttime yet. So Josie snuck upstairs again and came back down with as many books as she could carry—enough to last a good long while.

But once she'd stretched out in her fort with all of her books, she realized that the carpet wasn't as soft and comfortable as she'd thought it would be, so she tiptoed back upstairs yet again and brought down all her pillows to make a nice soft nest. She also brought down her boom box and some CDs while she was at it. After all, she might want to listen to some music. And she grabbed a flashlight to read once it got dark.

By now the fort, big as it was, was almost completely stuffed. Pretty much everything Josie owned or thought she might ever need was piled and stacked everywhere, so there was barely enough room for her to lie down. Her milk was warm, and not in the good way that comes from having Mom warm it up on the stove. The air in her fort felt stale and hot as late afternoon sun poured down on its

roof. Josie's graham crackers were stale, and truth be told, she was starting to feel lonely. But she'd never admit that. *Never.*

Finally, she couldn't stand it anymore. Back into the kitchen she crept, hoping to snatch an ice cream sandwich. Sneaky as she was, she couldn't get past her little brother and her mom, who were getting dinner ready. Spaghetti. Her favorite! Her mouth watered and her stomach grumbled, but Josie pretended not to even notice anyone else in the room.

"Madam President?" Mom said.

Josie stopped and cocked her head, wearing her haughtiest expression. "Yes?" she said.

"Would you like to join us for dinner?" her mom asked with a friendly smile.

"Well, perhaps I could join you this once. Like an ambassador," Josie said.

"We're having cockroaches for dinner!" Jeb exclaimed joyfully. Josie usually scowled when he said something gross, but this time, it was kind of funny, and she couldn't help but smile, with just one corner of her mouth.

After dinner, Josie's mom asked if she could see the fort. Josie agreed to give them a tour. It was too crowded with stuff for anyone to fit inside, so while her mom went to get some ice cream sandwiches, Josie pushed everything out except for her hamster and her pillows. Then, setting her most sparkly tiara delicately on top of her head, she escorted her mother and Jeb into her palace for dessert. The three of them had a lot of fun playing Kingdom. For once, Jeb totally cooperated with the game as Josie wanted to play it.

When it was time for bed, Josie's mother asked whether she was still planning to stay in there forever. Josie looked around her fort for a minute, and then said, looking shyly off to the side, "No, I guess not. No matter how big I make these things, I can't ever fit in everything I need."

"I know, honey. Come on, I'll tuck you in," her mom said. "You can clean this up tomorrow."

Fair enough. Cleaning up was worth being part of a kingdom that has spaghetti dinners, ice cream sandwiches, nice moms, and even little brothers who get their big sisters in trouble for things that aren't their fault.

DISCUSSION QUESTION:

Josie thought that hiding out in her fort would help her feel better, but in the end, she felt lonely. When she came back out, she had a new appreciation for her life just as it was. What things do you appreciate about your family and the life you share?

Permits, Please

CUBE CITY HAD BEEN Cube City for generations, centuries, millennia.

The City was governed by the firm hand of the Great Book, a vast data bank of thousands upon thousands of laws. There were so many laws that nobody could possibly remember them all. They were enforced by robot police who downloaded them, old and new, every night as the people slept.

The Great Book worked better for some residents of the City than others. While most residents of Cube City had round ears, sort of like we have, many others had pointy ears, like elves. These people were called Pointies, and the

Great Book had a lot of bad things to say about them.

Pointies had to do all the worst jobs. They were garbage pickers, boot polishers, snail herders, toilet cleaners. They were paid very little, never got any time off, and were treated badly by almost everyone. It was the Law.

One day, a young Pointy named Albert, who worked as a janitor at the Hall of Records where the Great Book was stored, had had enough. "Why do I have to chase the cockroaches out of the air vents all the time?" Albert fumed to himself. "I'm just as good at programming as Rexford is!" He said this out loud to the first robot policeman he could find.

"Permit, please."

"Excuse me?"

"Permit, please."

"What are you talking about?"

"Permit, please."

This went on for some time before the robot policeman finally explained that any Pointy wishing to complain must first obtain three signed and notarized copies of Permit #BH90210.

"Where, pray tell, can I obtain such a permit?" Albert asked.

"The office issuing Permit #BH90210 is closed until

further notice due to roosting bats."

Albert went home, took three aspirin, and thought and thought and thought. Then he slept on it as the robots silently downloaded the latest update to the Cube City Great Book.

The next day, he went to work as usual. He chased the cockroaches out of the cooling ducts, persuaded the giant rats to build their nests outside, and mopped up the sea-snail soup that round-eared Rexford had spilled all over his keyboard before taking his usual afternoon nap. Once Rexford started to snore, Albert tiptoed over to Rexford's desk and began typing quickly away on his keyboard.

Albert woke up the next morning, looked out the window, and smiled. Everywhere he looked, angry people with round ears were limping around gingerly in bare feet as stern robot policemen looked on. One round-ear was tussling with three robot policemen. Two were holding him by the arms while the third pried off his shoes.

"How dare you, sir! These are *my* shoes, by thunder!" hollered the man.

"Permit, please."

"What?"

"Permit, please."

And so it went. All people with round ears were only

allowed to wear shoes or boots if they had first obtained a properly notarized copy of Permit #227. The round-ears complained bitterly, but the Law was the Law.

The next day, as Rexford snored away, Albert typed some more, and yet more the day after that. And so it went. Soon, permits were required for virtually everything the round-ears did, and the robot police had never been busier. Round-ears required permits for eating toast at breakfast, wearing sunglasses, looking at the sky, saying "good afternoon," wearing the color brown, and even for whistling as they walked. Everyone agreed that the new laws were absurd, but the Law was the Law, after all.

A week or two later, Albert came up with his best idea yet, and the next morning, Cube City was very, very quiet. You see, the new law made it illegal for any round-ear to open or close doors or windows without a permit.

After enough time locked inside their houses, the round-ears finally began to understand just how foolish their blind obedience to the Great Book really was. After all, nobody knew where these laws came from or even if they did any good. Perhaps the Great Book was not infallible. Perhaps the Great Book needed to be changed.

Having overheard many round-ears finally talking sense, Albert entered one last law. The next morning, all the robot police were motionless and quiet. Some of the braver round-ears came out of their homes, and still the robot police did nothing.

"Do you like my new sunglasses?" they asked the stock-still robot police. "Boy, this toast is awfully good. Aren't you going to ask for my permits?"

"Robot police are no longer allowed to request permits unless they have previously obtained a permit to do so," replied one robot policeman. "Have a nice day."

And so the people of Cube City were free. They formed a Commission to Get Rid of Stupid Laws. Albert was the Chair, and the very first stupid laws they got rid of were those that decreed that people with pointy ears were to be treated any differently than people with round ears. From that time forward, Cube City was a welcoming place for all.

DISCUSSION QUESTION:
Rexford broke the rules of Cube City to try to change a system that wasn't fair. Is it ever okay to break the rules to try to create a better world?

How Raven Freed the Sun

This story was inspired by two Native American legends. The monstrous Wendigo comes from the mythology of the Algonquin people. There are many versions of how Raven "stole" the Sun, most of which come from the Haida and other tribes of the Pacific Northwest. I draw upon these characters and stories in a spirit of deep appreciation and gratitude.

THERE ONCE WAS A terrifying creature called the Wendigo. The Wendigo was thin and bony and had hot bright eyes that always gleamed, especially when it was hungry. And it was *always* hungry. It was the greediest, most selfish creature under the wide bowl of the sky.

What the Wendigo liked more than anything, though, was to smoke tobacco. The Wendigo smoked rolled-up tobacco cigars as big as evergreen trees. The smoke smelled awful and made all the animals cough. Now

tobacco has always been sacred to many creatures of
Earth and sky, but is to be used reverently, thoughtfully,
ceremonially. The Wendigo broke from all of these
traditions by smoking in a spirit of gluttony and greed.

Because of his huge appetite for rolled tobacco cigars,
the Wendigo wanted to grow the biggest tobacco plants
anyone had ever seen. He observed that his plants did not
grow during the night, when it was dark, but only during
the day, when the Sun was out. And so the Wendigo came
up with a terrible and cunning plan.

It climbed up to the very top of the tallest mountain,
and then up to the very top of the tallest tree that stood
upon the top of the tallest mountain. He was so close to
the Sun that he could see its smiling face. Although the
Sun's light was close enough to hurt his eyes, he stood
steadfast and called out, "Dear friend, dear Sun! Oh,
bright gift! I am so grateful to you for shining on my
tobacco plants that I would like to invite you to my house
for a feast."

The Sun, who had a kind and gentle spirit, felt deeply
honored. It wasn't every day that people climbed all the
way to the roof of the world just to say thanks. In fact,
the Sun was rather lonely, having only birds and clouds
for company most of the time. And so the Sun readily

accepted the Wendigo's invitation, and came down to Earth near the Wendigo's hut.

But it was a trap. The Wendigo grabbed the Sun and forced him into an enchanted box from which he could not escape. The Sun could not rise the following morning, and so the night did not end. All the plants and all the creatures of the earth were terrified.

The Wendigo did not care about the rest of the world, only about himself. He liked to carry the enchanted box back and forth through his vast tobacco fields with the lid partway open, just enough for the Sun's light to shine out on the plants every hour of every day. And the tobacco plants grew huge in the eternal daylight, even as all the rest of the plants of the earth began to wither away.

Soon, the Wendigo had more tobacco than he could possibly smoke, and he was feeling much too lazy to keep carrying the Sun box back and forth all day long. He set the box on a big rock in the middle of his fields so that it could shine on his plants forever without having to be carried around. After that, the Wendigo spent all of his time sitting outside his house smoking cigars as big as the world's tallest trees. And the smoke that blew out of the Wendigo's mouth made all the creatures of the world cough and choke and feel sick to their stomachs.

Meanwhile, the Sun felt weaker every day. He shined and shined and shined, but could never rise and never rest. Every day, his golden beams dimmed and weakened. The sad Sun was on the verge of simply being snuffed like a blown-out candle. And this was the Sun's sorry state when Raven flew by.

Raven was the most beautiful white bird in all the skies. In fact, he was so beautiful that all the other birds were jealous of him. Like all crows, Raven was a curious bird who loved all things bright and shiny. So when he saw the Sun shining like gold in the middle of the Wendigo's tobacco fields, Raven just had to fly down to see what was going on.

He was heartbroken when he got close and saw the Sun locked up and only barely glimmering. The Sun was too weak even to speak, but looking around, Raven could see what had happened.

"One second, O Brother Sun, one second and you will be free once more."

"Don't bother," the Sun whispered. "I am a slave now. I have forgotten how to rise. I no longer have the strength to shine upon the whole world. I can only remember how to sit here and make the tobacco grow tall. Just leave me be. I am not the Sun anymore."

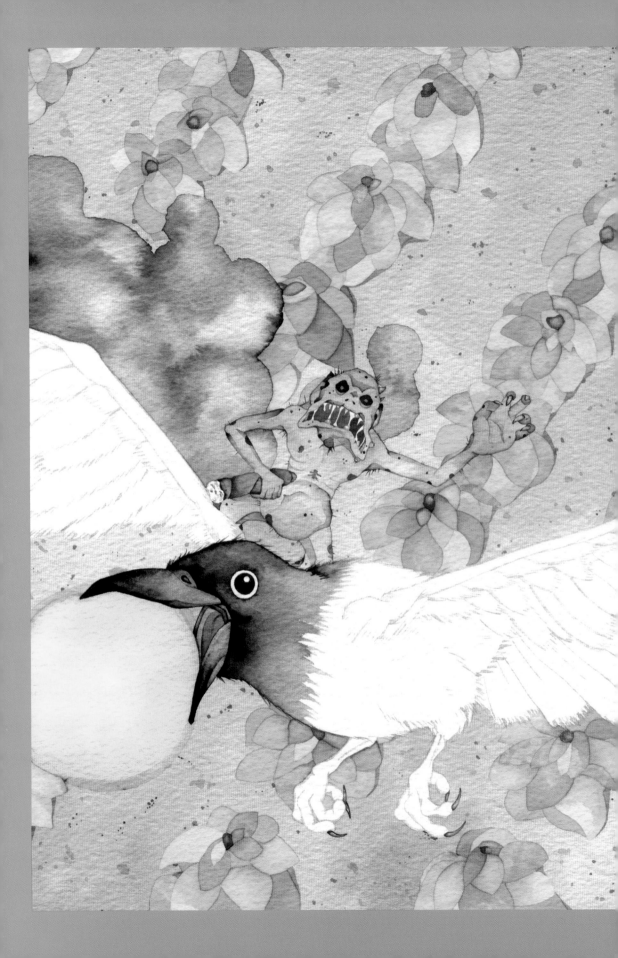

"Dear Brother!" exclaimed Raven. "The Wendigo made you forget who you are, but he can't *change* who you are. You are still the Sun, the bright, glorious life-bringer, the sweet-smiling creator of rosy-fingered dawn. *That* is who you are!" (Raven has always been known for his ability to turn a beautiful and encouraging phrase.)

As the Sun continued his weak protests, Raven stuck his beak into the box's lock and moved his head around until the lock popped open. The lid of the box flew off and Raven cried, "Rise, Sun, rise!"

But the Sun was too frail. He just sat in the box, feebly glowing.

Meanwhile, the Wendigo, hearing all the commotion, had come to see what was going on. As soon as he saw that the Sun's box had been opened, he roared and ran to lock it up again. There was no time to lose.

"Forgive, me, Sun, for my beak is sharp, but we have to get away," Raven said, and took the Sun in his beautiful white beak and flew up into the sky.

As they flew higher and higher, the Sun began to remember himself. Brighter and brighter he burned. "I remember who I am!" he cried out joyfully. Soon the Sun was so hot that Raven could not carry him anymore.

"I must let you go now, Brother," Raven panted.

"Yes, Brother Raven, I know," the Sun replied. "Thank you. *Now watch me rise!*" And with that, the Sun soared majestically up into the heavens, and all the world cheered.

Raven was thirsty from all his labors. When he flew down to a lake to get a drink, he was startled by his reflection. He was no longer white, but had been burned completely black by the Sun's rays. "Oh, well," Raven thought as he shrugged at his reflection in the water. "Black is always in fashion."

Ravens and crows have been black ever since. And the Wendigo hasn't been seen for many a year, because every time he so much as shows his face, the Sun shines at him furiously and gives him a well-deserved sunburn.

DISCUSSION QUESTION:
Just like the Sun, you have a special place and a special role in the world. It might be to help others, or to make art, or to learn in school. What is your special role in the world?

Squirrels vs. Blue Jays

GRANDPA JOHN AND GRANDMA Lillian lived in a little cabin way up in the forested hills above San Bernardino, California. Their three grandchildren, who they loved very much, came to visit them for part of every summer.

Saturdays were a big deal for John and Lillian, and they had all sorts of rules about what could and couldn't be done on that day of the week, which they called the Sabbath. They didn't use their cars on Saturdays. And they didn't cook any food, which the grandkids thought was pretty cool, because that meant they got to eat lots of peanut butter and jelly sandwiches. Saturday's meals felt like picnics. But no amount of peanut butter and jelly sandwiches could make up for the worst rule of them all: no television on Saturdays! No Saturday morning cartoons. No Saturday afternoon sports. No Saturday evening movies. Nothing.

The three grandkids loved to watch TV, so they didn't like that rule one little bit. They argued and complained. A few times, they even tried to secretly watch cartoons when they thought no one was paying attention, but Grandma Lillian had eyes like X-rays. She caught them every single time.

"Why do we need to follow all these rules here that we don't have at home?" asked the eldest granddaughter on a particularly lazy Saturday afternoon—an afternoon that would have been perfect for TV-watching. Instead, they sat outside on the big porch overlooking the back yard. A small creek ran right through it. Massive trees stood all around.

"Yeah. It's confusing!" moaned the younger granddaughter.

"Life's *boring* on the Sabbath!" said the grandson.

The three kids sat in glum silence for a while, looking out into the huge, overgrown backyard. The more the kids looked, the more little critters they noticed. There were lizards and muskrats and bunnies and mice and raccoons and birds of all shapes and sizes. But most of all, there were squirrels and blue jays.

And the squirrels and blue jays were at war!

Grandma Lillian had hung bird feeders all through the branches of those tall old trees. The blue jays were especially greedy birds and loved to chase all the smaller birds away from the feeders so they could hog all the birdseed for themselves. But the squirrels liked birdseed too—and they were even bigger than the blue jays!

The three grandkids sat on that back porch, caught up in drama every bit as compelling as anything on TV. The greedy squirrels raced along the top of the cabin and leapt all the way to the bird feeders, chasing away the blue jays in a flurry of blue feathers, squeaky squirrely war-cries and bushy tails; and then, just as the squirrels settled down to enjoy their ill-gotten gains, a whole squadron of blue jays dive-bombed in from the sky, squawking and whistling and chattering fiercely. And the squirrels would scatter like bowling pins as the blue jays tucked back into their birdseed feast.

And so it continued all day long. The grandparents came out and sat with their no-longer-bored grandkids.

"There goes old Silver Tail on another sneak attack!"

said the eldest granddaughter.

"I think Grandpa Blue Jay is getting fat," said the younger granddaughter.

"He won't be able to fly at all if he keeps eating so much," said the grandson.

When they got tired of sitting and watching, the kids made a map of the backyard, detailing where they imagined all the animals lived and how they fought over their jungle-like turf.

Then Grandpa John, who had been an actor when he was young, started a new game. He pretended to be a grumpy old man named Heinrich Schnibble who was always getting himself in trouble. He made up lots of stories about Herr Schnibble's efforts to get rid of the blue jays and squirrels in his back yard. The grandkids made up parts too, and then they all acted out the story.

Herr Schnibble fell prey to many funny pranks on that long Saturday afternoon. These stories—which almost always ended with Herr Schnibble shaking his fists helplessly at the blue jays and squirrels as they pelted him with acorns or stole his sandwiches—came to fill many of those long Saturdays.

That's how those grandkids came to understand why they had all those rules on Saturdays. The reason Grandpa

John and Grandma Lillian didn't cook or clean or run errands or let the grandkids watch TV was because for them, the Sabbath was all about family. From the time they all got up on Saturday morning to the time they all went to bed at night, the kids had their grandparents all to themselves—and the grandparents wanted the grandkids all to themselves, too!

If the day had been spent watching cartoons, this family would have missed the war between the squirrels and blue jays. And they definitely would never have met Herr Schnibble.

DISCUSSION QUESTIONS:

Does anyone in your family observe the Sabbath? What day does it fall on, and what special activities happen on that day? If your family doesn't observe the Sabbath, talk about how you might create one. What day would you choose? What would you do, and what activities would be off-limits?

Tippy the Cat

ONCE UPON A TIME, a kitten was born. He was a ragdoll cat, which is a very special breed of cat. Ragdoll cats have beautiful, long, luxurious fur. They are also famous for being the most mellow cats in the entire universe. These cats pretty much spend their days snoozing in the sun, snacking on dainty treats and making sure their fur looks absolutely fabulous at all times.

From the moment of his birth, this particular ragdoll was different. The rest of his family loved nothing more than to loll and doze in the sunshine, groom their soft fur, and be pampered by their humans. This kitten's eyes were always wide open and on the lookout. His fur was wild, sticking up in every direction, and when he walked you could hear him coming from a mile away—because unlike other cats, who walk silently, this kitten walked with short, powerful steps that sounded like drumbeats. While his brothers and sisters hung like wet noodles in humans' arms, he was stiff as a board and ready for action. Because he was so unsteady on his little kitten paws, his mother and father named him Tippy.

Tippy tried his best to fit in with the other ragdolls. He tried to hone his sleeping, relaxing and grooming skills. But the quiet life of a ragdoll was way too boring for him. He loved his family, but he was beginning to realize that he needed to find his own way in the world.

One afternoon, when he was almost grown up, Tippy heard the most amazing sounds he had ever heard. All the other cats were asleep, *as usual*, so Tippy quietly left the house and followed the sound. He found himself sitting on the sidewalk outside a stadium where a rock band was playing. He climbed up onto a wall for a better view, and he was mesmerized.

The music was as loud and as wild as Tippy's hair. The humans' clothes were just as wild as he felt: an anarchic blur of torn jeans, bright bandannas and eyeliner. It was the best thing he had ever seen. When the guitarist

smashed his guitar to pieces at the end of the show, Tippy
knew he had found his people.

He waited outside next to the tour bus, and when the
band came out and climbed in, Tippy followed right after
them. He climbed right up on the lead singer's lap, looked
him in the eye, and sneezed in his face. The singer, whose
name was Steel Tulip, laughed, wiped himself off and said,
"Man, this cat is rock 'n roll!" And that's how Tippy joined
a famous rock band called Blind Cheetah.

Tippy toured the world with Blind Cheetah. His
fur got bigger and bigger and wilder and wilder until

he looked like a giant grey furball with legs. Slam, the guitarist, laid his electric guitar on the stage and Tippy strutted back and forth across the strings, pulling on them with his sharp claws. Fans all over the world adored him.

Tippy sent his parents postcards from all the places he went: Tokyo, New York, London, Hamburg. They didn't understand his life, but they could see that he was happy, and so they were happy too.

After a few years of touring, Tippy retired from the band and went to live with two other cats named Pumpkin and Gabriel and their humans, Aaron and Eliza.

Pumpkin and Gabriel love having Tippy around. Knocking things over continues to be one of Tippy's favorite activities. He climbs onto the kitchen counter and head-butts the cat food container down, and then they feast when the container breaks open against the floor. He's way more mellow now, but he still loves to tell stories about his days with the band. Whenever he hears a good rock song, he starts bobbing his head, dancing around and looking for things to knock over.

Like every one of us, Tippy was born special and unique. He needed to find his own way in life, even if letting out his inner rock star sometimes makes his parents worry. Tippy loves mom and dad, but he didn't quite feel like himself until he grew up and left home.

This is something we all have to do as we get older. You might have years and years to be home with your family before the time comes for you to go to college or join a rock band or take off for New Zealand. But when the time comes, you'll be ready. And no matter how far away you go, you will always be safe and loved. You'll always be welcomed back. When Tippy goes to visit his mom and dad, they always welcome him with loud purrs and affectionate nuzzling.

If your time is now, then go. Have an adventure, grow your hair wild, and learn something about yourself that you never knew before. And if you ever see a miniature bright yellow muscle car cruising by, with dark tinted windows and tufts of grey fur sticking out here and there as an awesome sound system blasts music that makes the whole neighborhood shake, don't worry. It's probably just Tippy being Tippy.

DISCUSSION QUESTION:
It can be hard to encourage others when we think what they're doing is wrong—to trust that they know what's best for them. Adults, share a story about when this happened in your life: when you followed your heart despite the doubts of others. How did it all turn out for the best?

The Case of the Stolen Cookies

ONE NIGHT, PATRICK'S MOM baked Oatmeal Chocolate Chip Peanut Butter Monster Cookies. Her specialty. Not only did they taste awesome, they were huge—like a small Frisbee.

Patrick and his sisters *loved* those Monster Cookies. But Mom needed to take every last cookie in this batch to work for the big office party the next day. The smell of freshly baked Monster Cookies filled the house, but no one was allowed to eat even a single one. It was agony! Torture!

When the cookies were done baking and cooling, Mom

wrapped them up in a pretty box and tied a shiny green ribbon around it.

Sometime later that night, as the kids were watching TV in the living room, Mom burst in and turned off the TV with an angry click. One look at her face told them that somebody was in very deep trouble.

"Where are the cookies?" she barked.

Silence. "Where are the cookies? They were on the counter ten minutes ago and now they're gone! Where. Are. The. *Cookies*?"

"I don't know!" Patrick said. One of his sisters yelled, "I didn't do it!" The other sister protested "I was just sitting here watching TV!"

Mom looked at the three kids with tight lips. She said, "Go to your chairs."

Uh-oh. *The chairs.*

Patrick and his sisters went into the kitchen and pulled three chairs from the table out into the middle of the kitchen floor. Mom turned them so they were all facing away from each other. "You will sit here until *somebody* tells me what happened to those cookies," she said, and walked out of the room.

And so it began: sitting in silence in those hard wooden chairs for hours, potentially, until somebody confessed. They longed to be back in the cozy living room where their toys had no one to play with them and where they were missing the rousing conclusion of the cartoon they'd been watching.

"Just admit it, Dawn. You know you did it," whispered Patrick.

"Did not! I bet *you* did it!" Dawn shot back.

"Maybe Shelley did it," Patrick said. "I think I see some chocolate on her face!"

"You do *not* see chocolate on my face—it's on *your* face!" howled Shelley.

And so it went, mostly in growls and low angry whispers, for at least an hour. But as the clock continued to tick and it got later and later, and no one confessed.

Finally, Patrick switched tactics. "Okay, Dawn, maybe you didn't do it. But what if you just *say* you did? You're the littlest—you never get in trouble. But Mom's still mad from when I put that frog in Shelley's shoe last week. If I confess, I'll be grounded for a week! Come on…if you confess now, we can go watch TV for a little while before bed. Otherwise, we'll be here all night!"

Shelley had her own idea. "Dawn, if you say you did it, I'll let you sleep with Miss Bunny tonight."

Miss Bunny was Shelley's favorite stuffed animal. She

almost never let Dawn play with her. So, eventually, little Dawn gave in and confessed. Mom made Dawn sit by herself in the kitchen for ten more minutes while Patrick and Shelley ran off to watch TV.

Sometime that night, Patrick woke up. He sleepily went downstairs to get a drink of water and saw the kitchen light still on, even though it was very late. He peeked around the corner and saw Mom in her bathrobe, baking cookies. She looked very, very tired and very, very sad.

Patrick knew she had to get up early for work, and there she was, baking Monster Cookies.

"Mom?" he said. She jumped up, put her hand on her chest and smiled at him.

"Patrick! You startled me. What are you doing up?"

After a pause, he was able to say it. "It was me. I took the cookies."

"*What?*" She tossed her spoon down on the counter and turned to face him. Her smile dissolved.

His full confession tumbled out. "I tried to just sneak one out of the box while you were on the phone, but then I ruined the box and I knew you'd catch me, so then I took them up to my room and ate a whole bunch of them while Shelley and Dawn were watching TV." He took a big breath. "I'm really sorry."

"You ate a *whole batch* of Monster Cookies?"

"Almost a whole batch. Yeah." He sat down in a kitchen chair. "My stomach kinda hurts."

"Good," she said, and turned back to her bowl of batter.

"Mom, I really am sorry." he said. "Really, *really* sorry."

Mom nodded, and Patrick thought he saw a tear in the corner of her eye, which made him feel even worse. She went back to stirring the cookie dough.

Patrick stood there for a minute, then stepped up to the counter. Silently, he started to scoop the dough out onto the baking sheet in great big spoonfuls. They worked in silence, and by two in the morning, the batch was out of the oven and cooling on the kitchen table.

They looked sleepily at one another. Mom ruffled Patrick's hair like always. "Time to head up to bed," she told him.

"But Mom, I didn't get to eat the extra cookie dough…" Patrick stopped himself almost before the words were out of his mouth, and he and Mom laughed. "I guess I don't need to eat any cookie dough tonight."

"There'll be plenty of dough next time," she replied. As they started up the stairs, she draped her arm around his shoulders. The sleeping house was filled with the glorious smell of freshly baked cookies.

DISCUSSION QUESTION:

Patrick didn't really feel bad about taking the Monster Cookies until he saw all the extra work his mother had to do after he took them. Have you ever done something you knew was wrong but didn't feel bad about until you saw how it affected others?

A Town Called Driftwood

T HERE ONCE WAS A beautiful city called the City of
Sand, which rested alongside the wide Wet River. In
the surface of its still waters were reflected the incredible
buildings of the Sanders.

The Sanders, as you might expect, sculpted
everything out of sand. They dyed the sand in all the
colors of the rainbow: red, orange, yellow, green, blue,
indigo, violet. With their top-secret glue, they shaped and
molded the sand.

The City of Sand was beautiful. Towers, walls and
minarets glided to the sky in colorful sand-scapes. Sand
sculptures of ducks flew; sand water buffalo grunted and

sand-harps seemed to play themselves as the centuries rolled by.

The Sanders were artists. They were great artists, but they were not kind. Not to each other, and certainly not to the Dusters, who lived among the ruins on the high, dusty hill outside of town.

The Dusters rarely tried to make anything beautiful because they were too busy surviving, and they were very good at that. They could build a house out of just about anything. It was said that if they had to, they could even squeeze water from a stone.

For as long as anyone could remember, the Sanders lived by the river, building their great sand buildings while the Dusters did their best to survive in the dust. The Sanders looked down on the Dusters, of course, for being so dusty and simple. Dusters weren't even allowed to set foot in the City of Sand because they might dirty it.

But one year, just as the Harvest Festival arrived, the still river began to rise. The waters rose and rose for no reason anyone could see. Not even the oldest Sander or Duster had seen such a thing happen before. At first the Sanders found it amusing, but then, as the waters lapped at the sand walls at the edge of town, their amusement turned to fear. And then, the water began to spill over the edges of the sand walls like water from an overfull bathtub.

That's when the Sanders discovered something they really wished they'd known earlier: *The secret glue they used to hold the sand together dissolved in water!* Suddenly the whole City, that glorious sparkling rainbow of a City, began to collapse just as surely as a sandcastle collapses when the tide comes in.

The Sanders slept in the open for the first time that night. When they woke in the morning, the water had receded, but their City was gone. Where the river's edge had been rimmed with beautiful gardens and delicate walls of sand, there remained nothing but a huge, unsightly tangle of driftwood. The Sanders wept. "What will become of us?" they cried.

From above, the Dusters looked on, their faces unreadable. Some of them pointed down at the Sanders and held whispered conferences.

Then, in a large bunch, they came down the hill towards the devastated city. The Sanders didn't know what to expect. After so many years of having been treated cruelly, were the Dusters coming down to gloat?

Instead, the Dusters quietly divided into work parties by the riverside. They pulled apart the tangled driftwood and sorted it by shape and size. And then they started building.

Sanders may be snobs, but they do admire cleverness. They looked on in amazement as the clever Dusters began to shape that seemingly useless driftwood into simple, sturdy dwellings. They watched carefully, and soon they started helping out, learning as they went.

When the red sun sank, they worked straight on through the night by starlight. They worked the next day, too, Dusters and Sanders alike caught up in the thrill of building something new as a rebuilt city began to rise on the flood plain.

As the buildings rose sturdily, the Sanders came into their own, teaching the Dusters how to carve and decorate the wood so that it was not only sturdy, but beautiful. The Dusters were great at raw building, but they had never paid much attention to beauty. They had so much fun that they kept right on building even after there were enough houses for all the Sanders.

They finished just as the Harvest Moon began to rise in the east. The Dusters brought down all the food they had and threw a great harvest feast. Their foods were not spicy, delicate or syrupy like the fancy foods the Sanders loved, but all the Sanders' spices and syrups had been lost in the flood. Besides: an empty stomach and good company can make even the simplest food taste divine.

All together they feasted on seeds, roots, berries, and pancakes made of groundnuts as stories and songs passed like lazy birds through the night air.

The Dusters never left. It felt right to be together. And so they became one People and they named their new City Driftwood, so they would always remember where they came from.

DISCUSSION QUESTION:
Talk about experiences in your life where people have made choices to be unkind. How could they have made different choices?

The President Who Got Fed Up

THERE ONCE WAS A vast city on the African savannah known as The Great Burrow. It wasn't actually all that big by human standards, and it really wasn't so much a city as a big network of tunnels dug into the dirt. But for the creatures who lived there, it was most definitely a city—the biggest, most beautiful city in the world.

The creatures who lived there were meerkats, which are weaselly-looking mammals with white faces, twitchy noses and quick black hands and feet. Meerkats live together in giant families, and the meerkats who lived in the Great Burrow were the biggest family of meerkats in all of Africa.

Life was good for the meerkats of the Great Burrow—except for one big problem. Every spring, the wide river a few miles away rose higher and higher with the rains until it overflowed its banks and flooded the surrounding plains. The Great Burrow got flooded almost every year. In these floods, many meerkats were lost. Some lost their homes, and others fell prey to the terrible vultures that hunted the meerkats. With their tunnels flooded, they had nowhere to hide.

It was sad to live that way, but Spring floods were all the meerkats had ever known, and it never occurred to them that they might be able to do something about it…until Max the Meerkat entered the picture.

Every fall, the meerkats held an election to decide who should be the MIC (or Meerkat-in-Charge) for the coming year. It was really more a formality than anything, as the same sort of meerkat won the election every time: they tended to be the biggest, strongest, meanest and fiercest meerkats—the ones nobody ever wanted to challenge. So the MIC invariably turned out to be a domineering bully.

But one day, a new meerkat decided he'd like to give it a shot. His name was Max Meerkat. He wasn't the biggest or the strongest or the fiercest meerkat in town. In fact, he was kind of scrawny, but he was clever and good and always listened to what other meerkats had to say—even the littlest among them. And during the weeks before the big election, he told as many meerkats as he could that if he were elected, he would try to figure out a way to protect their city from the Great Flood.

Election Day came. Almost all the regular meerkats voted for Max, which was a lot of votes, but the biggest reason he won was because it never occurred to the big warrior meerkats that Max could possibly win. They didn't even bother to vote; they just stayed home and watched action movies. And so Max Meerkat became the new MIC. All the meerkats who had turned out to vote had a big dance party that night in the Great Burrow. Max was pretty psyched.

Days turned into weeks, and weeks turned into months, and everything was going great. All the meerkats thought Max was an excellent Meerkat-in-Charge, especially because he was so much nicer than the bullies they were used to.

The Spring rains were coming, and with them the floods. Max calmly resolved that he would find a way to prevent the devastation that threatened their city. He spent every afternoon walking around the Great Burrow, examining the river, and thinking.

One night he woke up with a brilliant plan. They would dig trenches to divert the floodwater. The river's overflow would flow through the trenches and around the Great Burrow instead of pouring into it.

The next morning, Max told all the meerkats about his plan to save the Great Burrow. Everyone was thrilled to have a new leader who was promising to change their lives for the better. He let them know that their help would be needed to make the plan work. "Hey, guys, we don't have much time left before the rains, and we've got a lot of digging to do," he said to as many kats as he could. "So I'll see you out there on Monday morning to help, right?"

"Yeah, sure, right, whatever," the other meerkats replied. "I gotta check my schedule, but yeah, I guess I could probably help for an hour or something before Meerkat Idol comes on."

Max spent the rest of the week drawing up intricate plans and gathering hundreds of meerkat-sized shovels and wheelbarrows and sandbags.

Everything was ready first thing on Monday morning, and not a moment too soon. Terrible purple clouds had already started to blot out the sun, and the air smelled like rain.

Max got up early and went out to the work site. He put on his hard-hat and waited, but nobody came to help him. He waited and waited. Finally, he started digging by himself, but one scrawny little meerkat couldn't even begin to do the work that needed doing. As he worked, the storm broke above him. Vast sheets of stinging rain swept across the savannah.

Max ran back to the Great Burrow. He found meerkats playing video games, watching TV and eating microwave popcorn, just like always! He tried to get them to come out to help, but no one would budge. Seeing their Meerkat-in-Charge rushing about, they just looked at one another and rolled their eyes, saying, "Well. He doesn't look very presidential."

Soon, the river began to flood. By the time the meerkats realized how much trouble they were in, the water had flooded many tunnels. Hundreds of meerkats were driven out into the stinging rain, where vultures waited for their chance to strike.

The terrified meerkats searched desperately for their MIC. They found him sitting on top of a hill overlooking the rising river.

"What do we do, MIC?" they clamored. "What do we do? We are drowning and starving and losing everything and the sky is thick with vultures! We thought you were going to save us! Isn't that why we elected you?"

"Listen," Max said calmly, the rain still pattering on his yellow hard-hat. "You elected me Meerkat-in-Charge, but I'm just an ordinary kat like the rest of you. I have lots of ideas and plans, but I can't make them come true without your help. It's not too late, and there is still time to save the Great Burrow, but we have to work together. We have to believe we can do this!"

The meerkats looked at one another. Their noses began to twitch with excitement and their eyes gleamed.

"So, can we do this? Can we save the Great Burrow?" Max cried.

"*¡Sí se puede!* Yes, we can!" all the meerkats shouted back.

Soon, they were all chanting together: "*¡Sí se puede!* Yes, we can! *¡Sí se puede!*" They raced down the hill after Max, threw on their yellow hard-hats, picked up their meerkat-sized shovels and got to work.

They worked for two straight days. Every meerkat pitched in. And then, just before the river flooded the whole plain completely, they finished digging the trenches. The floodwaters poured into them and away from the Great Burrow. Everyone was saved!

Things were different after that. Meerkats still went to Max for advice, but they didn't wait for him to take care of everything by himself. When a meerkat came to him with an idea about building a new school, for example, Max listened carefully before saying, "What a great idea! How can I help you with that?" And the very last thing he would say to his friends as they left to go build that new school or clinic was, "Can we do this?" and the reply was always the same: "*¡Sí se puede, Max!* Yes, we can!"

Max was re-elected many times in the ensuing years. Everyone agreed that he was the best Meerkat-in-Charge who had ever led their great city.

DISCUSSION QUESTIONS:
  Do you know of a big problem that needs solving? How would you offer to solve that big problem? What would you ask of others? How would you get them to help?

The (H)Edge of the World

T HE CUSTIS FAMILY WERE rabbits. They were Lops, a very special breed with super-soft fur and long, floppy ears that hang down and drag on the ground. Most of them were white with brown or black spots. They liked nothing better than lazing about in the sun and admiring their own gorgeousness.

For generations they had been living free in the Yard. They were never caged, because never once had any of them tried to escape. Why would they? They were fat and lazy and content. Except for Tilly.

Tilly was one of the younger Custises, and she was one of the most beautiful members of this large rabbit family. Her white-and-black-spotted fur was the softest, most luxurious fur anyone had ever seen. But Tilly didn't care one way or another about her looks. She was an *adventurer*.

Tilly was quite bored by her life in the Yard. Because of this, she found it hard to stay away from the Hedge—the one place the rabbits were forbidden to go.

The Hedge was at the very back of the Yard. It was a scraggly, dense, thorny hedge that was even taller than the humans. It was, the rabbits believed, where the world ended. Some rabbits said that terrible monsters lurked in its thorny depths, and that no rabbit who went there ever returned.

But Tilly found the hedge fascinating. *The Edge of the World!* Whenever her parents weren't looking, she hopped as close to the hedge as she dared. She cocked her head, listening for clues about what might lay beyond. And then, as the sun went down, she sighed and headed home for dinner.

One morning, everything changed.

Tilly had just woken up when the back door of the Yard screeched open. Within moments, two giggling humans had grabbed her with their huge pink hands. They made her play a terrible game they called "Dress Up."

Now, Tilly could live with them petting her, and she could even tolerate being held on their laps. But having them tie a shiny pink ribbon around her neck—well, that was just plain humiliating. When one girl tried to force a flowery hat over Tilly's ears, she decided to make a run for it.

She shot out of the girl's lap so quickly that the hat flew right off her head. The ribbon around her neck came loose and trailed behind her as the humans giggled and chased her all around the Yard, making a game of it.

Tilly was scared and very angry. She found a hiding place beneath an old car and crouched there, quivering. Her father had been watching, and as she tried to calm herself, he hopped over and spoke to her, not unkindly. "I know this game is no fun for you, but you must go back out there, dear. This is what it means to be a rabbit. They must have their fun or they will not feed us. Go, daughter, and do your duty."

Tilly wouldn't budge. "How *dare* they chase me like this? I am a rabbit, not a doll, not a toy, not a plaything! I deserve to have some dignity!" she fumed.

Even as Tilly protested, the girls sneaked up behind her and snatched her out of her hiding spot. Back on went the pink ribbon, the hat, and more. As Tilly gave in and went limp, something inside her shifted. She would never be the same.

The next morning, first thing, Tilly filled her cheeks with leftover salad and told her mother she was going on a long journey.

"And where might you be going, my dear?" asked her mother, who was distracted (as always) by her latest litter of pups.

"I'm going through the Hedge to the Edge of the World, Mother!" Tilly proclaimed.

Her mother, who was busy cleaning the face of one of her pink newborns, said nothing.

"Don't try to stop me!" Tilly went on. "I choose death before domestication!"

"Yes, dear. Well, have a nice time," Tilly's mother said, nosing the clean pup aside and starting in on the next one.

Tilly's ears turned red with irritation, but she said nothing more. It had been hard enough to say what she'd already said through a mouth full of partially chewed carrots. Fearfully, she hopped up to the dark, towering hedge. "Maybe this isn't such a good idea," she thought as she poked her head into the shadows. But brave Tilly kept going.

Thorns scratched her; strange, scary birds chirped at her; a large spider stared at her—but there were no monsters. She hopped more quickly now, more confidently, eager to see what the Edge of the World looked like.

Tilly finally poked her head through the last tangle of vines and gasped in wonder. There lay vast green meadow full of wildflowers and tall, leafy trees. The same sun beamed down, the same wind blew. And there were *rabbits* out there! They looked different from her—their ears were small and lay back against their bodies or stood up tall, and they were all shades of grey and brown instead of colorful like the Custises—but they were definitely rabbits.

Tilly hopped out into the meadow, stopping only occasionally to nibble on some unfamiliar but delicious plants.

"Hello there," said a young rabbit who was grazing nearby. "You sure are an unusual-looking rabbit."

"H-hello...What place is this?" Tilly stammered.

"Why, this is the Meadow, of course," the young rabbit responded. Like all the rabbits there, he was wiry and very athletic-looking. "I haven't seen you before. My name's Dustin."

"I'm Tilly. I came from over there. From the Yard."

Dustin seemed taken aback. "That's not funny! Everyone knows that that Hedge is the end of the world!"

"No, it's not," Tilly insisted. "I just came from there!"

"Don't even *joke* about that," Dustin said, obviously flustered.

But Tilly sensed that Dustin was an adventurer, like her. She coaxed him to the edge of the Hedge, and then into it. He followed her into the Hedge's mysterious depths and out the other side, into the Yard, where he gasped in awe at the manicured hedges and whitewashed house. He gazed upon the many colorful Lop bunnies, made some more new friends, and enjoyed all the salad he could eat.

And so, in one morning's time, the world of the rabbits got much, much bigger. Soon, skinny brown rabbits started showing up in the Yard for dinnertime salad, and Lop-eared rabbits raced across the open meadow, their ears flying behind them.

The humans tried to stop it, of course. They built a fence behind the hedge, but the rabbits burrowed under it. They set traps, which the rabbits ignored. They even tried to put the rabbits back in cages, but that didn't work either, because once a rabbit (or a person, for that matter) gets a taste of freedom, it's impossible to go back.

DISCUSSION QUESTION:

Think back on the scariest moment of exploration you've ever experienced. Share what you went through and what you learned.

The Stolen Hearts

JEREMY WAS IN SECOND grade, and so far, second grade had been no fun at all. Things weren't bad at school. He had some friends and got along okay. It was home that was the problem.

His mom and dad argued a lot. They tried not to fight so much when he was around, but sometimes at night, he lay in bed and all he heard was arguing. It was hard to sleep on nights like that.

One day, all the fighting stopped. His parents sat down with him and explained that they were going to get divorced and not live together anymore. They hugged him and told him over and over again that they both loved him so much, more than anything. Jeremy knew it was true. He knew they loved him, but he still felt very sad inside. A week or so later, Jeremy and his mom moved to a new town, just the two of them.

It was winter when Jeremy joined Mrs. Watson's class. Mrs. Watson was pretty nice, but everything else was terrible. Jeremy had never been outgoing. He was a quiet, shy sort of person. And because he was still so sad about his parents' separation, he was even quieter than usual. The other kids mostly ignored him. At lunch, he sat by himself, and at recess he just sat on the swing set and watched the other kids play. More than anything, he hoped that somebody would ask him to play, but nobody ever did. And Jeremy got sadder and sadder and sadder.

That's how things stood when Valentine's Day rolled around. In Mrs. Watson's class, everybody but Jeremy seemed to know that on Valentine's Day, everyone should bring cards and candy hearts to give away. So when Jeremy got to school in the morning, there were kids running around the classroom exchanging cards that said things like, "Be My Valentine!" or "Best Friends Forever!" Everybody was munching candy hearts. Some kids had piles of valentines so tall that they had to be divided into two stacks so they wouldn't fall over. But none of the cards were for Jeremy. His desk was empty.

Jeremy spent the rest of the morning feeling so lonely and sad that he wished he could just disappear. It was extra cold outside at recess that day, and after his ears started to tingle with cold on his lonely swing set, he remembered he had left his hat in the classroom.

He trudged back inside, pulled his hat off the peg by the door, and put it on his head. As he turned to leave, his gaze was caught by all those colorful little piles of Valentines and candy hearts.

And then, suddenly, without even understanding what he was doing, or why he was doing it, Jeremy started snatching the candy hearts off the desks and shoving them in his mouth. When his mouth was full, he filled his hands with the little yellow and pink and blue candies and ran down the hallway to the boys' bathroom. He went into a stall and sat there by himself, half-choking on all those candy hearts. Then, tears came. He tried to cry as quietly as he could so no one would find him there.

When the other kids came in from recess, they noticed right away that their candy hearts were gone. They were really mad that someone had stolen their candy, and when they realized that Jeremy was the only kid who was missing, they demanded justice.

Mrs. Watson gave the class some math problems to work on while she went to look for Jeremy. After looking high and low, Mrs. Watson heard muffled crying sounds coming from the boys' bathroom. She went in, and there he was, clutching a bunch of sticky candy hearts in each hand.

"Jeremy?" she asked. "Are you okay, honey?"

Jeremy looked up at her with his eyes wide and full of hurt, but he couldn't speak. He just cried harder. Mrs. Watson softly put her hand on Jeremy's shoulder and hugged him. His body began to relax, and then his hands began to relax, and all the candy hearts spilled out of his hands onto the floor.

After a while, Mrs. Watson asked, "Why did you take all the hearts, Jeremy?"

"I don't know… I just forgot my hat and then I saw all the cards and stuff on everyone's desk and my desk was the only empty one … and it made me so sad. Nobody likes me and I don't have any friends and that's how it will always be!" He was crying again. "*I just wanted some hearts.* I know I shouldn't steal. It was bad and I didn't mean it. I'm sorry. I just want to go home! I want to go home and never come back here ever again!"

Mrs. Watson hugged Jeremy some more, and she felt bad, because she had been so busy that she had never noticed how lonely he was. Jeremy was very upset and kept saying he wanted to go home, so she decided to call his mother to take him home for the rest of the day. As Jeremy waited for his mother in the school office, Mrs. Watson walked back to her classroom with a wrinkled brow.

Back in the classroom, she explained what had happened. At first the kids were angry, but Mrs. Watson asked, "How would you feel if you were new here, and didn't know anyone, and didn't have any friends yet or anyone to play with?"

The kids were silent. They hadn't thought about that before.

"And we didn't give him a card or anything," said one of the girls.

"Yeah. When we were doing our Valentine exchange, he was just sitting there, looking down at his desk," said one of the boys.

Mrs. Watson saw that the kids felt sad about how they had treated Jeremy, and so instead of continuing with regular class, Mrs. Watson and the kids got to work on something else.

The next day, Jeremy didn't want to go to school. He tried pretending to be sick, but his mom didn't buy it. She said, "Jeremy, I know you feel really bad right now, but you're going to have to go back there and face them sometime. You have to say you're sorry. Now you get on that school bus. I love you." She kissed him on the head, and off he went to school.

Jeremy felt very scared as he walked into Mrs. Watson's room. He shuffled over to his desk, looking at his feet. He was afraid to look up at any of the other kids, who he was sure were still mad at him. But as he reached his desk, he stopped short and gasped in astonishment. Right there, on his very own desk, was an enormous Valentine's Day card!

The card was made of fancy paper and decorated with sparkles and glitter. It was signed by every single person in the whole class. And in big red letters on the top of the page, it said: "To Our New Friend Jeremy."

When Jeremy looked up, everyone was smiling at him. A couple of the boys came up to his desk with a big plate full of red-frosted cupcakes with "Friends" shakily written on each one in white icing. Jeremy took one of the cupcakes and said "Thanks," so quietly that his new friends could barely hear him. He passed the plate on to

Peg, who was sitting next to him, and she took one and passed it on, and soon all the kids were eating the best cupcakes Jeremy had ever tasted.

They didn't all become friends right away, but it was a good beginning. Jeremy's heart hurt a little less with each passing day.

And from then on, whenever any new kids joined their classroom, or were moving away, Jeremy and the rest of the kids always made a special kind of surprise to welcome or to say goodbye. In honor of these occasions, they ate cupcakes that said, simply: "Friends."

DISCUSSION QUESTION:

Jeremy has feelings that push him to steal the other kids' candy hearts, even though he knows that stealing is wrong. Have you ever had the experience of being so mad, sad or scared that you can't help but do something you know isn't right?

Earth at the Interplanetary Conference

ONCE EVERY FIVE THOUSAND years or so, all the planets in our solar system get together for an interplanetary conference. They roast marshmallows in the warm glow of the sun, gossip about the other solar systems, and thoroughly enjoy one another's company.

The most recent meeting, however, was much more serious than usual. Earth was very upset.

"They used to be so cute and friendly," she said with a sigh. "They used to be so gentle. They used to thank me for everything they took—for the plants and animals they needed for food, for the rivers full of fish, for the gentle rains that watered their crops, and for the great trees they used to build their homes. They used to sing and dance to thank me, and sometimes I would sing with them. Oh, we all had so much fun back then! I used to love to watch them. So clever, those humans were, so full of invention. I couldn't wait to see what they were going to do next!"

"Well," intoned Neptune in his eerie-deep voice, "what's the problem, then? They sound rather delightful to me."

Earth sighed deeply and huge waves crashed against the shores of a thousand beaches. Great forests bent and swayed in a sudden violent wind that swept across continents. "I said, they *used* to be cute and friendly and polite. Now, they just take and take and take. They tear me up looking for gold and oil that they burn until my skies are black and smelly. Sometimes I think I'll never stop sneezing and coughing! They eat all the animals and bulldoze everything to make room for their cities. And you wouldn't *believe* how *messy* they are! They make incredible amounts of garbage and then just throw it in my oceans, or leave it laying around in great heaps. And they always want more, more, more! No matter how much they take, they're never satisfied."

She stopped for breath, and a single tear fell. It splashed into the Indian Ocean, where it quickly turned into a hurricane. "The worst part is that they don't sing to me anymore, and they never, ever say thank you. I just don't know what to do!"

All the planets were silent, except for Venus. Ever the lover, she murmured, "There, there, Earth. There, there," as she held weeping Earth close.

Mars, the mighty orange planet, spoke next. "Earth, as you know, I have some experience in these matters. You may remember the trouble I was having with those little green creatures that used to live on me—you know, the ones who called themselves Martians? They did the same thing to me. Their greedy tentacles grabbed up everything in sight. I gave them several opportunities to straighten up, but they didn't listen. So I sucked all the air and water back inside myself, and let the sun turn my skin into a giant burning desert. Those ungrateful Martians are all gone now, and good riddance. Tough love, I call it. If you want my advice, just shake 'em off like the fleas they are. Freeze them with an ice age, drown them in floods. You'll soon forget they were ever here."

Some of the planets nodded, especially Saturn, who always seemed to be in a sour mood. The two smallest planets just looked sad. Earth saw their distress and asked, "What do you think, little ones?"

Mercury, who is much more shy than you would think, simply blushed. But tiny, icy Pluto spoke up.

"Earth, I am so sorry for your pain," she said softly. "The way they are treating you is terrible. But look at me. I float alone in space, just a big block of ice. No one has ever sung to me. As I drift along through eternity, I dream that someday I will be able to share myself with others. I dream that one day I will be needed, that I will be able to feed creatures of my own and watch them grow and thrive. But it seems that is not meant to be. Not for me.

"But so many creatures depend on you, Earth, even if they forget how to treat you, how to sing to you, how to thank you. Maybe they can learn. Maybe they can grow up. Please be patient for just a little longer, Earth."

"But maybe Mars' solution is the best one," Earth said. "I can't wait forever for those foolish humans to start behaving themselves!"

"I don't think brother Mars is as happy as he pretends," Pluto continued as Mars gruffly wiped away a big red tear. When the other planets looked his way, Mars grumbled, "I'm not crying. I just got a bit of space dust in my eye…"

Earth asked Pluto, "Then what do you think I should I do?"

"It might be time for *you* to sing to *them*," whispered Pluto.

And so Earth began to sing as she had not sung for a very long time. It was a song of creation, of love and promise, of warm earth and cool water, of fresh spring grass and deep forest. She sang of buffalo and beaver, of fern, sage, and willow. She sang of dolphins and mountains and people. Yes, she even sang of people; despite their behavior, she still loved them dearly.

The Earth sang, and nearly every living thing swayed and leaped and sang with her. But most of the humans could not hear her song. None of them heard it, in fact...aside from a handful of children.

When the Earth let her voice soar fully into her song, a few children in each nation stopped what they were doing. They heard the Earthsong as if it were coming from someplace deep inside their bodies. These children could hear the song of the trees, the flowers, and the whales in the ocean. Suddenly they felt like singing too. They sang with strange smiles on their faces. Their mothers and fathers and teachers and friends said, in their own native languages, "What on Earth has gotten into you?"

And in their own native languages, these children said things like:

"Mom, I don't think we do a very good job with our recycling."

"Dad, I don't think I need a ride to school anymore—I'll start riding my bike."

"We don't need to throw these food scraps in the trash. Let's start a compost pile in the backyard."

"For this birthday, instead of having people bring me presents I don't really need, let's ask for donations to a charity that helps to clean up the environment."

"Let's try growing some more of our own food instead of buying food that comes from hundreds or thousands of miles away. Let's use our reusable bags and walk to the farmer's market for whatever we don't grow ourselves."

The mothers and fathers and teachers and friends asked, "What's bringing all this on?" And the children, still humming to themselves, didn't really know. "I just remembered something important," they answered.

Earth smiled, and everyone in the world suddenly felt a warm breeze, as gentle as a mother's hands, lifting their hair and touching their faces.

DISCUSSION QUESTION:
What more would you like to do to take care of the Earth?

The Bagheads

EVERY YEAR, TWO NEIGHBORING villages got together on a sunny afternoon for their annual soccer match. The players took this yearly tournament very, very seriously.

Teams were comprised of the mayor and city councilors from each village. One year, not so long ago, The Mayor of Huddleston and his team totally destroyed the Mayor of Wiggleby and his team, eight goals to one. The Mayor of Wiggleby and his village Council were very upset and embarrassed. And, as people often do at times like these, they started looking for someone to blame.

Many people whose families originally came from Huddleston had ended up settling down in Wiggleby. Many of these families had now lived in Wiggleby for generations, but the Mayor said it was all *their* fault that the Wiggleby team had lost. "If all those ex-Huddlestonian Wigglebys had cheered for us properly, we would have won for sure—but we all know they were secretly cheering for Huddleston. For this, they must pay," he proclaimed.

And so the Mayor and the City Council of Wiggleby issued an edict: From now on, anyone whose family had ever lived in Huddleston must wear a bag over their heads from that day forward. Nobody from Wiggleby would be permitted to have anything to do with them.

The Mayor kicked off his new initiative by stepping down from the lectern from which he'd been proclaiming and addressing a small boy. "You there, child, your grandfather was a Huddleston man, wasn't he?" he said, not harshly.

The boy nodded.

"I thought as much!" snarled the Mayor, startling the poor child. "Now, you must wear this bag as your due and just punishment!" And he slid the bag down over the child's head, just like that.

The next day at school, a handful of children sat in class all by themselves with bags over their heads. Nobody sat with them at lunch. Nobody was allowed to play with them on the playground.

But Jillian couldn't bear to see her best friend Claudia sitting all alone with a bag over her head, so Jillian put a bag on her head too. Once she'd hidden her non-Huddlestonian face from view, she was free to go and sit with Claudia.

By the end of recess, tons of kids had bags on their heads. Nobody could tell who was who. It was chaos! The Mayor was furious, and was about to have all the bagheads arrested to teach them a lesson. But when the police chief arrived at his office, he had a bag over his head, too!

The Mayor ran outside. Everywhere he looked, he saw a sea of people with bags over their heads, coolly going about their business.

Seething with anger, he hurried home for dinner. There, in his wife's chair, was a strange woman with a bag over her head. In his old sainted mother's chair was another strange woman with a bag over her head. And in the little high chair where his little daughter Emily usually sat, there was a giggling little baby…with a bag over her head!

Nobody was going to make the people of Wiggleby turn against their friends and neighbors, whom they regarded as sisters and brothers. Some people even carried homemade signs that read:

I Might Be From Huddleston!

Finally, the Mayor and his Councilors were the only people in town who didn't have bags over their heads. They began to feel foolish—and they also began to feel lonely. After they rescinded the Edict, the people of Wiggleby forgave them; but first, they demanded that the Mayor and his Councilors wear bags on their heads for a whole week…so they would know how it felt.

To this day, all the people of Wiggleby keep their bags hidden carefully away, just in case anyone else ever tries to divide them.

DISCUSSION QUESTION:
Have you ever risked getting in trouble or done something you would rather not do because you wanted to support someone you cared about?

Be Careful What You Wish For: A Halloween Story

ELIZABETH AND HER FAMILY had just moved to a new town—a small town that felt very different from the big city she had lived in since she was a baby. It was perfectly nice, but Elizabeth was worried. Would her new school be harder than at her old school? Would she make friends as good as those she'd left behind? Luckily, she had one really special friend—a super-soft, fuzzy, playful orange kitten named Pumpkin. Elizabeth spent hours playing with Pumpkin every day. They even slept together at night. Whenever she needed a friend, Pumpkin was right there, purring happily at the privilege of being with her favorite human.

Elizabeth was tall for her age and excelled at all kinds of sports and games, but her favorite thing to do was climb trees. As summer waned and school approached, she spent many hours climbing the trees near her house. She was lonely and worried, but being in the trees always comforted her.

On the very first day of school, they had Field Day, where all the kids ran races and went through obstacle courses and climbed ropes and shot free-throws and all that sort of thing. Elizabeth was awesome: She was the fastest kid in her grade and won almost all of the races—she even set a new school record for rope-climbing! She was proud of herself, which helped her feel brave enough to start trying to make new friends.

But after her Field Day triumphs, everyone she tried to talk to was mean to her. The boys, who seemed embarrassed to have been beaten by a girl, chanted "Tomboy! Tomboy!" whenever they saw her. They even pretended she smelled funny—which she didn't! And the girls were no better. When Elizabeth asked them to play foursquare with her, they turned up their noses. "No, we only like to play girl games—like house and Barbies—with *real* girls, not tomboys."

Elizabeth felt terrible. She decided that the only way she would be able to fit in at her new school would be to prove to everyone she was no tomboy. She'd show them she was a "real" girl.

When Halloween came, she chose a beautiful pink princess gown for her costume. She combed her hair neatly and tied it with a shiny pink ribbon. Her outfit was very uncomfortable compared to her usual jeans and T-shirts, but when she looked in the mirror, she had to admit that she looked just like a princess. Even so, just before she left to go trick-or-treating, she felt fear creep into her belly. What if the other kids were still mean to her, despite her beautiful costume?

Tears welled up in her eyes. She looked into the mirror through her tears and said, "I wish this wasn't a costume. I wish I really *was* one of those princess-y girls!"

What Elizabeth didn't know was that this particular mirror, which they had found in the attic of their new home, was old and powerful. It was a magic mirror, and without her ever knowing, it granted her wish. Still feeling pretty much like herself, she went outside.

Just then, a roll of thunder cracked in the sky. It was getting very dark. A storm was coming! She saw a

bunch of kids standing around the giant oak tree near
her house. Elizabeth ran over to the old tree and saw
that way high up, in the topmost branches, was her best
friend—Pumpkin! Pumpkin must have been scared into
the tree by the thunder. He had climbed way too high and
couldn't get down!

No one seemed to have the courage to climb up
the big tree. Elizabeth, who had always been a master
climber, took a running start and jumped for the nearest
branch—but she couldn't reach it. She tried again.
The thunder was getting louder. Within minutes, the
storm would be upon them. But her body felt strangely
weak and uncoordinated, as if she had never climbed
a tree in her life! She tried and tried, but she just
couldn't do it.

And then Elizabeth heard a voice inside her head. It
said, *"Princesses don't climb trees."*

With a shock of recognition, she ran back to the house
as fast as she could and went right up to the mirror. "I
don't want to be a princess!" she shouted at her reflection.
"I just want to be me!" Suddenly she felt much, much
stronger.

She raced back out to the tree and climbed up,
reaching her poor, trembling kitten in the blink of an eye.

From branch to branch she hopped, swung and leapt
with incredible agility, always moving, never fumbling or
looking down. Once she had scooped Pumpkin gently
into one arm, she descended deftly, but carefully, without
a moment's pause. Only as she hopped down from the
lowest branch did she realize that all the other kids were
staring at her in amazement.

"Nobody's ever climbed the big oak before," said one
of the boys. "How'd you get so good at climbing trees?"

"I've had lots of practice," she answered. "I can give
you some tips sometime if you want."

"Cute kitten," said Suzy. "Can I pet him?"

"Sure," Elizabeth answered.

They all crowded around her and petted her now-
purring cat. No one even noticed Elizabeth's princess
gown, although it was a little dirty and torn from
climbing. The storm blew over, and they all went trick-or-
treating together.

Most kids stopped being mean to Elizabeth after
that. And even when people did call her a tomboy,
Elizabeth didn't care. She liked herself just as she was.
She didn't need to wear a costume or pretend she was
somebody else.

But sometimes, just for fun, she still puts on her dress

and wears it around. And although she prefers jeans and a T-shirt, she often ties her hair into a ponytail with that shiny pink ribbon...just because she likes it.

DISCUSSION QUESTIONS:

What are some things you are good at? Do people sometimes seem jealous or intimidated by how good you are at certain things?

Brave Raven

THE STORIES OF RAVEN'S adventures are full of bravery, fortitude and derring-do—especially the ones he tells about himself. Don't get him started, or he'll tell you all about how he stole the Sun and set it in the sky for all of us to share. And then, with barely a pause for breath, he'll go on for *hours* about the time he outsmarted the greedy Wendigo. One thing he's *not* likely to tell you, however, is the fact that he hasn't always been brave.

When Raven was tiny, he lived inside an egg, like all his brothers and sisters. It was warm and quiet and safe, and he liked it in there. But he kept growing bigger and bigger every day. Soon enough, the egg began to crack.

Through that growing crack, Raven could see the world outside: a sky so brightly blue that it hurt his eyes and trees so tall they made his stomach lurch. The sounds of all the chattering birds and animals of the forest sounded mysterious and threatening. It was chaos out there! Raven decided that he would *never* leave his wonderfully warm egg, no matter what.

He curled himself into a tight ball, making himself as small as possible. But he kept right on growing anyway and whenever a bit of egg would crack off, he desperately snatched at it with his beak or his claws to pull it back in place. After a while, his egg no longer really looked like an egg at all; more like a jigsaw puzzle of an egg with a bunch of pieces missing. Forlorn-looking black feathers poked through the cracks.

While Raven's brothers and sisters broke free from their eggs, stretched their hungry beaks, and learned how to fly, Raven kept himself busy by snatching up bits of their shattered eggs to patch the ever-widening cracks in his own. Months passed, and frightened Raven still shivered inside the remains of his egg with his big feet poking out through the bottom. He slurped worms through a hole that he closed up again after every meal.

When Spring came, Raven found himself surrounded

by a new batch of eggs, which eventually hatched into a new generation of blind and squawking family members. He added yet more bits of shell to his own, ever-expanding egg, poking his beak out only to gobble the worms delivered by his devoted mother.

But a family of burly, brawling, bullying blue jays had recently moved into the neighborhood. They hid in the trees watching the nest, and whenever Mother Raven dropped off some worms, the jays swooped triumphantly in and greedily gobbled them up. The baby ravens were too little to stop them, and Raven was still pretending to be an egg, so the blue jays got fatter and fatter and the baby ravens went hungry. Raven still loved his egg, but his heart lurched whenever he peeked out through a chink in his shell at his hungry brothers and sisters.

And so it was that one morning, after the jays had thumped into the nest with all their rude chatter, after they had begun to slurp up worms like spaghetti noodles while the baby ravens cheeped in weak protest, Raven could stand it no longer. Something had to be done.

Before he knew what he was doing, Raven took a deep breath and stood up. He drew himself up to his full-grown raven height, stretching his wings menacingly. Hundreds of bits of eggshell scattered around him like rain. He fixed his bright eyes on the biggest of the jays and gave a booming, croaking caw:

"LEAVE…THIS…NEST. *NOW!*"

Now, a full-grown raven is a huge bird, much larger and scarier than any blue jay; and here was one who had appeared out of thin air, as if by magic! Of course, those rude, cowardly jays panicked, stumbling over one another in desperation as they dove away from the nest as fast as they possibly could.

"Hip, hip, hurrah, big brother!" the baby ravens peeped. "You're our hero!" Raven was so proud of himself that he forgot all about his egg, which now lay in shards on the ground beneath their tree. He divided the worms among his tiny brothers and sisters, saying, "Please, don't mention it, really, it was nothing. Just part of the job, part of my master plan. I was just waiting for the moment when you all needed me most…"

And soon after that, Brave Raven flew away into the wide, wide world for a life full of adventure.

DISCUSSION QUESTION:

Raven finds his courage when he sees the big, mean jays stealing food from his brothers and sisters. How do you find your courage when you're scared?

You Can't Stop the Music

THERE ONCE WAS A Kingdom called Warble, far
away across the seas. Warble was named after
its inhabitants, who were funny-looking creatures who
looked sort of like gnomes. But unlike the gnomes most
of us have seen, the Warbles were covered from head to
toe with soft feathers, like baby ducks. Because of these
feathers, they were known far and wide as the Fuzzy
Warbles.

The Fuzzy Warbles were the most musical of
creatures. There was rarely a moment when they weren't
singing, and even in their sleep, they hummed. They had
beautiful, clear-throated voices that sounded like a blend

of human voice, birdsong, and clarinet.

Fuzzy Warbles never developed speech, so anything they had to say to one another, they said through song. Even simple phrases like "Good morning!" or "Take out the trash, please," or "Don't miss your school bus, dear!" hummed with beauty when sung by a Fuzzy Warble.

And so it happened in that charmed place that the Old King passed away and a New King ascended the throne. The New King was an unusual Fuzzy Warble in that he did *not* have a beautiful singing voice. Try as he might, his voice came out sounding like a cross between a duck and a frog. He was deeply ashamed of this, although he never admitted it.

So the very first thing he did when he became King was to issue a Decree of Silence, making it a crime for any Warble to sing. From that moment on, they were to communicate only through handwritten sticky notes.

Singing was so deeply built into the Fuzzy Warbles that they could not stop singing, no matter how hard they tried, and the jails overflowed with sad Warbles who had broken the No Singing law. Once imprisoned, however, they had nothing more to lose, and so the halls of every jail resonated with their sad and beautiful music.

The King then paid a sorcerer from the far side of

the mountains to come and silence the Warbles for good. The sorcerer stood on top of the highest tower and cast a terrible spell that pulled the Warbles' voices right out of their bodies. The captured voices were slowly pulled from them up into the air, where they drifted together into a pale golden mist. This song mist wafted across the city and into a big clay jar, which the sorcerer then corked up and gave to the New King, who was to keep the jar in a secret spot in his opulent sleeping chamber on the seventh floor of his stone castle.

The Fuzzy Warbles looked at one another desperately and tried to sing, but no sound came out. The whole city was buried in silence.

After that, the only sounds were the sounds of working. Life in the city had become plain and hollow and sad, and the whole world seemed covered in sticky notes.

One day, a little Warble names Curtis was washing up the dishes from lunch. Without realizing what he was doing, he began tapping a spoon against a pot, *tap, ping, tap, ping*. Suddenly, doing the dishes seemed a lot more fun. Before he knew it, he was plinking the glasses, making swishing sounds with the water, and using the soup spoons like drumsticks on the sink.

All across the city, Fuzzy Warbles stopped what they

were doing and listened. They listened, and then they began tapping their feet. Then they started tapping, swishing, shaking, and blowing whatever was around them. It was contagious! Soon, the city was a symphony of blowing reeds, blacksmith rhythms, tinkling glass, zipping washboards, and stomping feet. In a matter of minutes, every Warble in the land was dancing. Except for one.

Alone in his high palace, the King heard the unmistakable sound of music and threw open his windows in a rage, ready to arrest the whole town if necessary. But he couldn't see anything unusual. Nobody was singing.

All he could see were Warbles going about their usual business—plowing, blacksmithing, cooking, fetching water, washing dishes and clothes. Nothing unusual about that—except that those Warbles seemed to be having a lot more fun than they were supposed to!

The King stood there on his balcony for a long time, and as he gazed suspiciously down upon his people, a funny thing began to happen.

One of his fingers began to tap on the balcony rail. How strange! Then one of his feet started tapping, all on its own. A few seconds later, the New King was surprised to find his head bobbing, and that was just the beginning. It was as if his body had been taken over by the Spirit of Music. Soon, he found himself banging a powerful rhythm on an old suit of armor and moonwalking across his balcony like Michael Jackson. Although his voice wasn't much to listen to, it turned out that the New King had the gift of rhythm! Soon, the walls of the great city were literally shaking with the music of life. The New King couldn't stop laughing.

A huge smile on his face, the King picked up the clay jar where all the Warbles' voices were stored. He lifted it high above his head and threw it down from the balcony, where it shattered with a resounding crash. A shimmering golden cloud rose up above the dust, and as the Fuzzy Warbles breathed in, every voice found its way home. A more beautiful thing could scarcely be imagined.

Many years have passed since then. The Fuzzy Warbles still sing, but they also play all the other kinds of music they discovered during the Great Silence. The King is the best drummer in all the land, and it has been a dog's age since even a single sticky note has been seen in the Kingdom of the Fuzzy Warbles.

DISCUSSION QUESTIONS:

Have you ever felt jealous when someone else has been good at something that you're not good at? Did it make you want to stop them from doing that thing? What strengths do you have that other people admire and wish they had, too?

Winter Solstice: The Bottom of the Well

TRISTAN GRUNTED AS HE helped his father heave the huge and heavy green Yule log into the hearth. He was pretty big for a boy of thirteen, but the log was as big as he was. The thick green log would burn smokily for several days. There would be itchy throats and coughing because their chimney was in sore need of a good cleaning.

Still, even with the coughing, this was one tradition that Tristan's family celebrated every single year, as they had for generations. They lit the huge Yule log on the shortest, darkest day of the year, late in December, and they kept it lit until the whole log was reduced to ash.

Because the log was so big, this could take days, and the whole time the family and their neighbors would celebrate, day and night, in a giant party full of food, drink, singing, storytelling...and smoke.

Truth be told, Tristan was not looking forward to the Solstice. Because he was the oldest, he'd have tons of extra chores to do: chopping wood, taking care of the sheep, fetching water. You name it, Tristan had to do it. And then, when he finally got done with all his chores, he couldn't relax even for a minute because their cottage was full to the brim with his baby sisters and brothers, who never seemed to stop crying except when they were hogging all the attention from the grownups. That, plus the smoke that made him cough, plus the feeling of being invisible because nobody seemed to know he was there except when they needed something fetched, chopped or carried...it all made Tristan wish the whole stupid Solstice would just be over before it even began.

So, once the Yule log was lit and the babies started crying and cooing and being cute, Tristan snuck out of the cottage to be by himself.

He felt lonely and resentful as he roamed out across the moors. Even though the sun was setting, Tristan

walked farther and farther across the pastures. He thought
he would check on the sheep. At least *they* always seemed
happy to see him.

Tristan eventually found the herd in one of the farthest
pastures, by the old homestead his great-grandparents had
lived on. They only looked up for a moment when Tristan
arrived, then went right back to munching the frosty grass.
The sheep might not have been the friendliest of creatures
or the best conversationalists, but at least they weren't
squalling and pooping their pants all the time like the
babies back home. It felt good to just sit on the old stone
fence and watch them eat.

After a while, though, his ears perked up at a half-
heard sound. It was hard to make out, but it sounded
almost like a baby crying. It was a high, distant sound that
made Tristan shiver; he feared that it might be one of the
ghosts said to walk these moors at night, especially around
the Solstice, when the veil between the worlds is thin.

Afraid as he was, Tristan couldn't help but be curious.
It couldn't be a baby, he thought, *not out here.* But what
if it was? What if a small child had wandered away and
gotten hurt? There were lots of old wells and hollows and
caves out here that could be dangerous for anyone who
didn't know their way.

Tristan slid off the wall and set off to find the source of the sound. He was still a bit afraid, but now he also felt brave, like a hero from the old songs. Even if he did meet a ghost, he would not back down—although he did wish he had thought to bring some salt in his pocket. (Everyone knows that the thing to do upon meeting a ghost is to throw salt at it. Ghosts are compelled to stop and count every single salt crystal before they can do anything else.) That would have given Tristan plenty of time to get away. But, alas: no salt.

The sun was definitely setting now, and the sky was getting dim. It was early in the day, but this was the shortest day of the year—the day that darkness chases the sun away and takes over.

Tristan followed those high, sad, echoing cries across the moor until he saw one of the old wells in the distance. The well was so old that nobody remembered who had lived there, or when. It was really just a crumble of ancient stones set in a falling circle. You wouldn't even know there was a well there unless you stopped to look inside. But the sound seemed to be coming from that very spot.

Tristan started running. If someone had fallen in the well they could be badly hurt, or maybe even drowning! He reached the wall, threw himself down on its edge, and looked down through the murky gloom, panting. And he saw a small white blur at the bottom of the well.

The small white blur was bleating and crying like a newborn baby. It was a lamb. A baby sheep that must have wandered away and fallen.

Poor thing! It sounded so afraid. Without a thought, Tristan started looking for a way down into the well. He had to rescue that lamb!

The walls were very slippery. He found a few handholds and footholds to help him get down, but then he slipped and fell. Down, down he plummeted, all the way to the bottom of the well. He landed with a cold splash next to the lamb, which stood up to its knees in ice-cold water.

Shocked by the water's icy chill, Tristan jumped to his feet. He grabbed the lamb around the belly and began searching for handholds to climb out again, scolding the lamb the whole time for being such a stupid baby. But the rocks were too slick. Try as he might, he could not climb out.

Great, he thought. *Now we're both stuck down here. Stupid baby lamb*!

Tristan yelled for help, but he knew it wouldn't do any good. He was far away from the cottage and hadn't told anyone where he was going. Everybody would be preparing for the big feast right about now, and the cottage would be full of singing and music and cooking food. Nobody would hear him. It was starting to get cold indeed now, and shivering, wet Tristan was truly scared.

He was just starting to cry when the lamb nuzzled him with its wet nose. The lamb was wet too, but its coat was soft, even warm, like a pair of wet wool socks. Tristan hugged the lamb close and they both felt a tiny bit better.

Night fell. The stars began to come out. Tristan could see them reeling and dancing high above him, casting the only light in his world. He could only see a small circle of sky from the bottom of the well, but somehow, the stars seemed warm and comforting. Aside from the soft breathing of the now-sleeping lamb, Tristan had never felt so alone if his entire life, and his heart ached.

He just stood there in the shin-deep water with that lamb in his arms, gazing up at the black and twinkling sky, thankful that his feet were staying dry in his winter boots. At some point he must have fallen asleep on his feet.

With a jolt, he opened his eyes to the sight of a bright star field. It took him a few moments to realize that his head was on his chest and he was looking down

at the reflection of the starry sky in the water at his feet. Tristan laughed out loud at the thought that he was standing with his feet in the sky amidst the moon and the stars. It was so beautiful. He looked up at the real sky, and back down at the mirrored sky reflected at his feet. Although he still felt very much alone, he also felt strangely peaceful. He thought of his family back in the hot, smoky cottage telling jokes, clapping their hands and stamping their feet to Old Uncle's pipe and whistle songs. He thought of his mother's well-worn face and strong hands; he thought of his red-cheeked father's powerful shoulders and always-aching back. Tristan thought about all his family and neighbors, and even about his little sisters and brothers—who, at that moment, were probably drowsing off with a faint crust of sugar stuck to their faces.

He remembered how his little brothers and sisters looked up at him as if he were the only person in the world, the only person who could help them sit up in their heavy blankets or hold a spoonful of broth for them to drink. They knew they could count on him to blow on the broth so it wouldn't be too hot. He remembered what it was like to get up for chores early in the morning when only the birds were awake, so early that when the sun came up it was almost blinding. It soaked into his skin and hair and eyes like liquid gold.

Tears ran down his cheeks. They were tears of loneliness, but also love. He hugged the sleeping lamb closer—even though his arms were aching terribly after so many hours of holding that woolly little body close to his own.

In time, the black of the sky at the top of the well grew less black and the stars began to fade. He was jolted out of a half-asleep daze by the distant sounds of shouting.

"Triiiistan!!!!" the voices rang out. "Tristaaaaan!"

His heart beating hard in his chest, Tristan opened his throat and yelled as loud as he could—so loud, in fact, that the lamb woke up abruptly and began bleating too. Soon, Tristan heard the crunch of approaching footsteps, and then he saw his father's worried face looking down at him from above. "I found him!" his father cried. "Tristan, are you all right?"

Tristan nodded, unable to speak.

"I think he is unhurt…he's fallen in the well!" his father told the others as they gathered around. A long rope dropped down, and Tristan tied it around his waist. Then, Tristan's father and mother and uncles and aunts and neighbors—who had all been out looking for him all night long—hauled him up out of the well with that little lamb still firmly in his arms. As he rose, the sky got bigger and bigger and bigger. And as he emerged, the world seemed unspeakably vast.

Once out, Tristan was almost knocked over by rib-cracking bear hugs from everyone. All mashed together like that, the family looked like a large, strange animal with arms and legs and beards sticking out in all directions. Tristan's cheeks were soon wet with everyone's tears of relief, which mixed with his own.

In all the hugging and crying and laughing and bleating, nobody noticed the shining gold disc of the sun rising swiftly and unstoppably over the hills and fields. It wasn't until they were bathed in the warm light of morning that a silence overcame them. There they stood, the whole family, with their faces turned toward the rising sun. It had come back, yet again, after this long, dark night.

They turned to head back to the cottage, before they had gone more than a few steps, Old Uncle started up with a tune from his whistle, and it became a parade all the way home. By the time they got there, the sun was full up, and the Yule log was still burning merrily in the smoky cottage. Tristan had never felt so happy. His mother brought him a bowl of hot stew and Tristan began to gobble it down. Then he paused.

"It isn't lamb, is it?" he asked.

"No, dear," his mother said, and everybody laughed.

DISCUSSION QUESTIONS:

Did you know that the Winter Solstice is an ancient celebration of the shortest day of the year—the day when the sun rises late and sets very early? The Summer Solstice is the longest day of the year. How are the Solstices celebrated in your world?

Tristan feels like he has too many responsibilities. He realizes, once he has fallen into the well, that he likes being responsible—that his sisters and brothers and parents appreciate him for his contribution. What are your responsibilities in your family?

It's important to feel appreciated for the responsibilities you take on. Take a moment to appreciate each other for all you do to keep everyone in your household safe, healthy and happy.

The End of Beavertown

NOT SO VERY LONG ago, there was a place called
Beavertown. Beavertown was a series of three or
four ponds connected by lots of secret underwater tunnels
and channels. As you might guess, the reason it was called
Beavertown is because it was home to lots and lots of
beavers.

Beavertown was old. Really old. Beavers had been
living in Beavertown for longer than anyone could
remember. It was a great town, with lots of big green trees
for eating, fish for chasing, and underground dens to keep
warm in the winter and for raising baby beavers. There
were birds and mountains and flowers and pretty much

everything a beaver needs for a happy life. And there were even some humans around: a couple of farmers, a few houses and an old man who sometimes used to fish in the beaver ponds. Everyone got along, for the most part.

But one morning, all the beavers woke up to find that the water in their ponds was draining away! This was just about as bad a thing as could happen in Beavertown.

Some of the bravest beavers volunteered to go exploring to see where all the water was going. They were gone for a whole day and a night, and when they came back, all the other beavers gathered around to hear what they had to say.

The returning beavers looked very sad and scared. Their whiskers drooped with exhaustion. They told their beaver friends that they had traveled far, far away, farther than any beaver had ever gone, but just when they were about to give up and turn back, they had found the new farm.

This farm wasn't a farm like the others that dotted the valley. It was huge, with big buildings, bright lights, and lots of noisy machines. Vast fields surrounded the farm, and gigantic metal pipes shot water over all the plants. Lots and lots of water.

That was where their water was going. It was being

sucked up by the big metal pipes that led to the farm!

Now, all living things need water, but beavers need water even more than the rest of us. They live in it, get their food from it, and play in it. Without water, they will die. So you can imagine how upset all the beavers in Beavertown were that night. Some beavers were crying. Others were angry and wanted to try to chew through the metal pipes. Still others just sat there, shocked and confused. The beaver children were scared too, because they had never lived in a world without water. Many had never seen their parents so panicked.

Nobody slept that night. The next morning, the sky was grey and the beavers saw how dried-out their beautiful town was getting. Some of the beavers started acting very strangely, walking around Beavertown saying things like, "Woe is us, the end is near!" and, "Prepare for the final hours, beavers, we are being punished for our sins!" Nobody had ever heard such talk before, but to many beavers it seemed to make sense. How else to explain why their town was being destroyed? Maybe they deserved it.

More and more beavers started gathering around to listen, and before long, lots of beavers were shouting and crying. Some just sat down and waited for the world to end.

Old Grandmother Beaver, the oldest beaver in

Beavertown, spent most of her days basking in the sun on a big old tree stump outside her den. Most beavers were a little scared of her because she was so old and tough. She didn't talk much, when she did, she spoke her mind. One day, in the midst what most of Beavertown thought was the end of the world, Old Grandmother Beaver left her stump and walked right into a circle of beavers who were tearing at their whiskers and chanting, "The end is near!" As she gazed at each beaver with her fierce old eyes, they fell silent one by one. One beaver said tentatively, "Welcome, Grandmother. Have you come to wait for the world to end?"

She silenced him with a fierce stare and thumped her tail loudly on the ground. "No, I am most certainly not here to wait for the world to end!" she barked. "I'm here to talk some sense into all you silly beavers."

"But, Grandmother, can't you see the water is gone? This is a sign that the end is here! We can't live without water."

"Oh, pish-posh! Do you think we have never been without water before? Do you think we have never struggled and suffered?"

The beavers thought about this for a moment. One spoke up: "We have. I can remember the winter when the waters froze so hard and many of us died."

Another said, "I remember the times hunters came with guns and traps and killed us for our fur."

Other beavers spoke of their pup-hoods, of going hungry, of being afraid and uncertain when they did not know how they would make it through. But they had. They had made it through because they loved one another. Their parents had not been willing to give up on life and hope while they were just helpless babies. They made it through because beavers have always stuck together and kept living as best they could even when it seemed hopeless. Some of them had died, yes, and many had suffered, but Beavertown had lived on.

"Listen to me, beavers," Grandmother boomed. "The world has always been like this. The water comes and goes. Sometimes, we grow fat; other times, we go hungry. Terrible things happen, and we don't always understand why, and it can seem like the world is ending. But we have faced trouble before, and look—we're still here! I know it is scary for you, but we must keep going, keep living, keep trying." Old Grandmother Beaver looked slowly around the circle. "We can't give up. So, who will volunteer to go find us some new water? An undisturbed group of ponds, perhaps, or a private swamp?"

The crowd was silent for a few seconds. Then, one

small beaver thumped her tail on the ground and said, "I will go!" And that's all it took. Soon, everybody was thumping and shouting and dancing around, chanting, "I will go! I will go!"

That very night, four groups of beavers left Beavertown. One went north, one went south, and the other two went east and west. They were gone for seven days and seven nights. Meanwhile, the water in Beavertown dwindled almost to nothing. Everyone was very worried, but they held on to hope, did what they could, and took care of their pups. Finally, at dawn on the seventh day, a group of very tired beavers stumbled wearily into town and said, "We found it." Then, they promptly fell asleep.

The beavers set off to their new home that very day. And there, they are still building dams and chewing bark and fishing and playing and living. Together, they learned that just because things look bad, it doesn't mean the end of the world.

DISCUSSION QUESTION:

When the beavers think that their water is going to disappear, they don't know what to do until old Grandmother Beaver reminds them that they have overcome trouble before and they can do so again. In your world, what troubles have been overcome when things seemed hopeless?

The Story of Dog and Duck

THERE ONCE WAS A dog who loved ducks. Rather, there once was a dog who loved *one* duck.

The dog's name was Willow, and she lived in a nice small house with a minister, his wife, and three cats. One of Willow's favorite places to hang out was the beautiful garden right across the street from the church where the minister worked. They spent a lot of time over there, walking on the trails and exploring secret paths.

Willow's favorite part of the park was the big pond where turtles sunned themselves on warm rocks and big orange koi fish swam in the cool green waters. Most of all, she loved to watch the happy ducks bobbing on the water, doing their duck-ly things: dunking their heads all the way down so that their tail feathers pointed straight up at the sky, grooming their feathers, quacking, running and flapping their wings along the pond's surface to take off for a flight, splashing down when they were done, and napping with their heads tucked beneath one wing.

One day Willow was snarfling around by the edge of the pond. She was so busy smelling all the good smells that she almost head-butted a duck that was standing on the edge of the pond looking at her. The duck was a mallard, with a beautiful shiny green head and a bright beak.

Willow was curious about the duck, and the duck was curious about Willow. Willow barked her friendliest bark, and the duck gave his wings his friendliest flap. In no time at all, they became the best of friends.

That night, when the minister and his wife tucked Willow into bed, she said, "Poppa and Momma, I am tired of being a dog. I think that tomorrow, I will become a duck."

"Hmmm," the minister's wife said. "Are you sure that's what you want to do? Being a dog looks like a lot of fun to me."

"I don't know, Momma, a dog's life is okay, I guess,"

she said drowsily, "but I bet it's way cooler to be a duck." With that, she drifted off to sleep.

The next morning, Willow woke up early and headed over to the big pond for the first day of her new life as a mallard duck.

"Good morning, Duck," she said to her friend the duck.

"Good morning, Dog," her friend replied.

"Hold on, Duck, I'm not a dog anymore. I'm a duck just like you," said Willow.

Duck bobbed his head and said, "That's cool. Want to go for a swim?"

"Sure!" Willow exclaimed, and jumped in with a big splash.

The two ducks, one sleek and feathery, and the other big and furry, had a lot of fun for a while. They swam and chased flies and splashed around, and even chased after bread crumbs thrown from the shore by excited kids, who had never seen a duck like Willow before.

But soon, Willow was completely exhausted from all that swimming. Every time she tried to climb up on the shore to rest, Duck cried, "Come on Willow, ducks don't rest on land! We rest on water! We do *everything* on the water! Come on back in, the water's great!"

"What about sleep?" Willow asked.

"Why, we sleep on the water, of course. It's very relaxing."

"Oh," Willow said, trying to sound enthusiastic. Meanwhile, she thought: *Maybe I'm not cut out to be a duck after all. I like to sleep on my comfy brown pillow. I'm not turning out to be any good at quacking, and flying seems to be out of the question.* Then, she had a terrific idea.

"Hey, Duck, have you ever thought of becoming a dog? It's pretty fun to be a dog. And then we can hang out all the time! We can be best friends forever!" she said to Duck.

Duck took to Willow's new idea right away, and cried out, "Why, yes! I always thought I would make a good dog. See, look what I can do." Duck wagged his tail-feathers awkwardly, making a strange quacking sound that might have been the bark of a small, wet dog with a bad chest cold. Still, Willow was impressed, and told her friend so.

Dog and Duck galloped back to the minister's house, where they rolled around in the dirt and sniffed and snarfled at all of Willow's favorite places. Duck was a little embarrassed to tell Dog that carrying around one of the

minister's socks, or munching on a rawhide bone wasn't really all that fun. But the real trouble began when the feathery and furry dogs decided to play Willow's favorite game: Chase the Cats.

The cats, you see, were not the least bit amused at being chased by a small, feathery, duck-like dog. In the blink of an eye, poor Duck was being chased through the house by three angry cats, while Willow ran along behind, shouting: "Hey! You cats! Leave my friend alone, you big bullies!"

Duck waddled and flew at top speed all the way

back to the pond, where he came in for a landing with a splash. Cats, of course, don't like water at all, so they gave up the chase, licked their chops with disappointment, and went home.

Willow sat forlornly by the pond's edge.

"I'm sorry, Dog," Duck said as he rolled some water down his back, "but I don't seem to be cut out for life as a dog any more than you are cut out for life as a Duck. Maybe we can't be friends after all."

"I'm sorry too, Duck. I'm sorry my uncles chased you like that. They can get pretty grumpy sometimes."

They sat in silence for a short while, Dog lolling in the dirt and Duck enjoying the cool caress of the water and the koi nibbling at his toes.

"You know what?" Willow said. "I think we can still be friends, best friends, even though we're so different. We can hang out right here, all we want. You can swim and I can snarfle! It'll be great! Friends, Duck?"

"Friends, Dog!" Duck quacked. They did a paw-to-wing high five, and the minister managed to snap a picture.

Dog and Duck are friends to this very day. Willow still keeps her copy of the high-five photo taped to the wall above her food bowl. Duck had his laminated, and he keeps it under his favorite sunken log next to his tadpole collection.

The next time you are in that beautiful garden having a walk or a picnic with your family, you might see them: a big golden dog and a green-headed duck, chatting away happily at the edge of the big pond, enjoying a grand friendship despite their differences.

DISCUSSION QUESTIONS:

In their friendship, Willow and the duck each learn new things. Willow learns what it's like to act like a duck, and the duck learns what it's like to act like a dog. Do you like to try new things? What have you tried lately that you'd never tried before, and what did you learn?

The Rainbow Bridge:
A Chumash Story

THE NATIVE AMERICAN CHUMASH people were created on Santa Cruz Island, which lies like a jewel just off the coast of southern California.

Legend has it that the Chumash were made from the seeds of a magic plant by the Earth Goddess, whose name was Hutash. Hutash was married to the Sky Snake, which was the name the Chumash people gave to the swirl of stars we now call the Milky Way.

Hutash could make lightning bolts with her tongue, and one day, she decided to give the Chumash people the gift of fire. She stuck out her tongue and a bolt of lightning leapt from her mouth, starting the very first fire.

After the wife of Sky Snake gave them fire, the Chumash people lived more comfortably. More people were born each year, and their villages got bigger and bigger. The island was getting crowded. The noise the people made was starting to annoy Hutash, and it kept her awake at night, so she decided that some of the Chumash would have to move off the island to the mainland, where there weren't any people living in those days.

But how were the people going to get across the water? Hutash thought on this for a long time, and then decided to make a bridge: a very long, very high rainbow that stretched from the tallest mountain on Santa Cruz Island all the way to the tall mountains across the sea. Hutash told the people to go across the Rainbow Bridge, and to settle there, and to fill the world with people.

As the bridge stretched from the island to the mainland, Neela and her little brother Anacapa played on the beach, without a care in the world. Neela was collecting beautiful shells with which to make necklaces and bracelets while Anacapa swam and played in the white waves.

Although Anacapa was younger than Neela, he was already a great and fearless swimmer. He was so quick that he could catch fish with his bare hands, while everybody else had to use spears and nets. But for all his talent, little Anacapa was also a reckless and disobedient boy with a knack for getting himself into trouble. So Neela, who was older and much more mature, always kept a watchful eye on him.

Their Grandmother explained that they must leave the island with the rest of their family and many other people from their village. The children were sad, for they had never been anywhere else, and could not imagine a more perfect place. Still, they obediently followed their grandmother back to the village. Their heads hung low, and their eyes said silent goodbyes to all the rocks and trees and hills they knew they would never see again. But everything changed when they saw the Rainbow Bridge.

Everyone was astonished to see this enormous bridge stretching all the way across the sea toward the dark mountains at the edge of the world. The bridge arched high into the sky, much higher than the tallest tree, and it was so long that no one could see the end of it. Neela and Anacapa quickly forgot their sorrow when they gazed up and through the Rainbow Bridge's shimmering colors: red, orange, yellow, green, blue, indigo, violet in the bright morning sun. It was the most beautiful thing they had ever seen.

Many people were afraid to step onto the bridge. After all, they could see right through it, all the way to the crashing waves far below. It was scary to think about climbing up into the sky on a rainbow and walking across the ocean to a strange new place where they didn't know anyone, not even the names of the trees.

But the goddess had been very clear. They must cross the bridge, and everybody knew better than to argue with a goddess! So the Chumash people started along its great curve, stepping up and out over the glimmering blue sea.

As Neela and Anacapa stepped onto the hazy

watercolor bridge, Grandmother warned them, "Do not look down, and do not look back. You must walk straight ahead and keep walking. Promise me that you will do as the goddess says!" The children looked at Grandmother's solemn eyes and promised.

Some of the people began to worry and fret as they left the only home they had ever known. They wanted to look back at their homeland. Others, like Anacapa, started to feel so sure of themselves that they became careless. Time and again, Neela caught her little brother trying to look down through the bridge out of the corner of his eye. She slapped him on the head and said that he must keep his promise to Grandmother and the goddess.

But in the end, Anacapa's curiosity got the best of him. He dropped a stone onto the bridge to see what would happen, and it fell right through. Down and down and down it fell, until it hit the water far below with a tiny splash.

Suddenly, he was terrified. How could the bridge hold him when it couldn't even hold a small stone? Anacapa fell to his knees, staring down through the bridge to where the stone had fallen.

Others had seen the stone fall too. Some managed to stay calm and to keep their eyes straight ahead, and they got across safely. But many flew into a panic and made the terrible mistake of looking down. They just couldn't help it, and so they fell.

It was a long way down from the Rainbow Bridge. Down, down, they fell, through the fog and into the ocean far below.

Neela saw her brother fall. She screamed and lunged toward him, but her grandmother caught her firmly by the hand and forced her to keep walking.

Many were falling now, and the goddess Hutash, looking down from the sky, felt very badly about this. She didn't want them to drown. She looked at Anacapa falling down, down, down like a stone, and, with the wave of her hand, she turned Anacapa into a dolphin.

He splashed into the water and, almost immediately, began to flip and frolic quite happily. Pleased with herself, Hutash transformed the rest of the falling Chumash people into dolphins with another graceful twist of her hand.

Neela and the rest of her family made it across the bridge with Anacapa swimming along behind. For many years after that, Neela and Anacapa continued to play on the beach as they always had, Neela collecting shells while her brother danced on the waves. And this is why the Chumash still believe that the dolphins are their sisters and brothers.

DISCUSSION QUESTIONS:

Anacapa was told not to look down while he crossed the Rainbow Bridge, but he couldn't help himself, and he fell into the sea. Have you ever been told not to do something and did it anyhow? What did you learn?

Bee Strike

THERE ONCE WAS A President whose favorite thing in the whole world was peanut butter, banana and honey sandwiches (which he called PBB and H for short). He had eaten them since boyhood, but in those days, his parents used to make him eat other things too, like broccoli.

On the day he became President, he said to his mother, his father and all of his advisors, "No. I will not eat broccoli. I am the President of the United States of America, and I will eat whatever I please…and I wish to eat PBB and H sandwiches!"

Less than a month later, the President's chef had a

nervous breakdown from making nothing but peanut butter, banana and honey sandwiches all day long. But the President would not be denied. He had a whole bunch of engineers from NASA design a special robot whose only job was to make PBB and H sandwiches, just the way the President liked them.

Soon, peanut butter, banana and honey sandwiches were a national craze. Everybody wanted to be like the President, and that meant eating what the president ate. It started with the members of Congress, who demanded that only PBB and H sandwiches be served in the cafeteria. Then, they changed the name of the sandwich, which they all felt took to long to say, to "Freedom Food," which they thought had a patriotic ring.

Soon everybody was eating Freedom Food, because if they didn't, people might think they were against America. In glossy magazines, on television, and in newspapers, supermodels, sports stars, and pop stars were captured mid-PBB and H, grinning at the cameras with their faces full of peanut butter and their fingers sticky with honey. And once the President, the politicians and the celebrities started doing it, then *everybody* in America started doing it. All the peanut farmers in Georgia started buying expensive cars and building enormous mansions.

But there was one really big problem. The bees couldn't keep up.

Those hardworking bees just couldn't make enough honey for everybody in America to eat peanut butter, banana and honey sandwiches every day. When they complained, the President just demanded that they work a little harder.

So they worked in shifts around the clock. They closed all the bee schools so the little-kid bees could go to work in the honey factories. They abolished weekends, so there were no more Saturday morning cartoons or bumblebee soccer leagues. To make room for more honey storage, the bees were forced to exile all those who were too old or sick to work. Still, no matter what they tried, and no matter what strict new rules the President laid down, the bees simply couldn't make enough honey for all those sandwiches.

One day, a worker bee named Cesar decided that enough was enough, and called a meeting of the hive. Hovering up in the air where all the bees could see him, he said, "This is no good, my friends! We cannot go on like this. We are living like animals, but we are *not* animals! We are *bees*, and we deserve better! We deserve to send our children to school, to go to the doctor when

we get sick, and even to have some time to relax and be with our families. It's time for everyone to stop taking us for granted and to start treating us with the respect we deserve!"

The bees buzzed very loudly, which is how bees cheer, and they hoisted Cesar the Bee onto their bee shoulders and started to put his plan into action.

The first thing they did was stop making honey. Every bee in the hive simply flew off the assembly line. Other bees flew to the other hives, and soon all those hives stopped working too.

Right about this time, the President received a strange postcard in the mail. On one side was a list of all the bees' demands—health care, education, better working conditions, vacation time and so on—and on the other side was a picture of a peanut butter, banana and honey sandwich with a big red 'X' through it.

The President was furious. He sent soldiers to take over the hives and force the bees back to work. But the bee lookouts, who were stationed all around, saw the soldiers coming. By the time the soldiers had surrounded the hives, all the bees were gone. (Some say that the bees' good friends the hummingbirds showed them the secret way to the fabled Hummingbird Hideout.)

The American people tried to go on living and eating as they always had, but it was getting harder to find honey anywhere. Everyone was upset, and famous celebrities were photographed throwing tantrums at expensive restaurants after learning there was no honey on the menu.

The President, being rich and powerful, did have honey for a while, long after all the rest of America was going without. Eventually, though, even the giant White House honey pot was empty. The President was worried, but he was not quite ready to give in to the bees' demands.

And then one night, the President came home after a really bad day, during which the President of Russia had made fun of his new suit, the Premier of Uzbekistan refused to let him use their country as a landfill and the King of Sardinia called him a creep! Whenever the President had a terrible day like this one, the only thing that made him feel better was a big triple dose of Freedom Food: three fat peanut butter, banana and honey sandwiches piled one on top of the other! But, alas: there was no honey.

The President raged. He bellowed! He threatened! He even held his breath until his face turned purple. Still, no honey appeared. Finally, he broke down and wept, right there in the Oval Office.

"Fine! I give up!" he sobbed, blowing his nose into the curtains. "Get Cesar the Bee on the phone right away. Tell him they've won—they can have their stupid weekends. They can have their dratted health care and their precious schools. They can even take some seasons off every year. Let them have whatever they need...but get me a peanut butter, banana and honey sandwich. RIGHT NOW!"

And so it was that just a few hours later, photographers crowded and jostled to snap the now-famous photograph of the President of the United States shaking forelegs with Cesar the Bee. Cesar smiled at the cameras and said, "This is a small step for one bee, but a giant step for all bee-kind!"

And that is why bees only work during certain seasons, pollinating certain plants at certain times. It is also why peanut butter, banana and honey sandwiches are not as popular as they once were, now being served only on the most special of occasions.

DISCUSSION QUESTIONS:

Sometimes we think that if other people—especially, people we think are cool, or interesting, or popular—are doing something, we should do it too. Does that happen in your world? What does it feel like to want to do something just because it's the popular thing to do?

Cesar the bee gathered all of his bee family and friends and persuaded them to strike, which means that they refused to work until they were treated better by the people they worked for. They were able to peacefully get what they wanted by cooperating with each other and agreeing on what they would ask for. In what other ways can we get our needs met without fighting?

Summer Camp Blues

IT WAS NATHAN'S FIRST time at summer camp. In fact, it was Nathan's first time away from home overnight, period, and he was nervous. He was a shy boy, and sometimes it was hard for him to make new friends. And there he was, surrounded by strangers, sentenced to a whole week at Bear Lake.

At breakfast that first morning, it seemed like he was the only one who didn't have any friends yet. Almost all the other boys knew each other. Some knew each other from home. Others had been coming to Bear Lake for a long time and had made friends, and they greeted each other happily as Nathan looked on.

But he made it through the first day well enough. He chopped firewood, shot arrows at the archery range and went swimming in the deep green lake. As he drifted off to sleep in his bunk that night, he thought, "Camp might be fun after all." But the second day did not exactly meet his criteria for "fun."

Nathan was one of the last boys to wake up. By the time he made it to the cafeteria, there was nothing left to eat but oatmeal, which he hated with a fiery passion. As he faced off with his bowl of rapidly coagulating slop, boys all around him were digging into plates heaped with bacon, scrambled eggs and pancakes with maple syrup. He couldn't bring himself to eat even one bite.

When he got up to throw the oatmeal away, a bunch of kids ran past, bumping into him and knocking his bowl out of his hands. Oatmeal splattered all over his shirt and pants. Suddenly, it seemed as though every boy in the whole place was laughing at him. That's how, on only his second day at camp, he got a nickname: Oatmeal. And from that point on, things only got worse.

Later on, Nathan was out on the lake. He canoed happily along, having temporarily forgotten his troubles. No one had called him Oatmeal for at least an hour. When he saw a big fish swimming by, he stopped paddling and leaned over the side to take a look—and his glasses slipped off of his face and into the deep, deep water.

"Oh, NO!" he gasped. "Not my glasses!"

For as long as he could see his glasses—which wasn't long, because he could hardly see without them—he mournfully watched them drift toward the mucky lake bottom. Then, there was nothing to do but turn the canoe back toward the shore, which now looked like a long, blobby blur.

He was hungry.

He was pretty sure he HATED camp.

Dejected, Nathan docked the canoe and walked back toward his cabin. At least he *thought* he was walking back toward his cabin. Because he couldn't see without his glasses, he took the wrong path and was soon totally lost. A few minutes later the sky turned purple and a cold rain started to hammer down, soaking him almost instantly. He couldn't believe it. "What is GOING ON!?" he hollered.

He ran towards a big tree on the other side of the meadow, hoping to at least get out of the rain. On the way, he tripped over a rotting log. The ground where he fell was soft, fortunately, but when he sat up, a large, black cloud began to rise up right in front of him. A large, black, *buzzing* cloud.

"No, no, no, no, no!" he yelled as he took off across the meadow at top speed, hotly pursued by a swarm of angry ground hornets.

Nathan ran and ran. But every time he looked back, that buzzing cloud seemed to be right on his heels. He came to an old woodshed and crashed through the door, slamming it behind him. And then he just sat down and cried.

"I wish I never came to this stupid camp!" he yelled to no one in particular. "I hate it, I hate it, I *hate* it!"

It took a long time for him to stop crying, but when he did, he heard a wet, snuffling, rustling sound. There was something in the woodshed with him! Sure enough, in the back of the shed, under an old bench, was a small grey rabbit. One of its legs was caught in a rusty old trap. Its coat was spotted with blood and its eyes were glassy.

Nathan pried apart the jaws of the trap, but the poor thing just lay there, its breath fast and shallow. It was in bad shape. Nathan ripped his t-shirt into strips and tied a few around the bloody leg to stop the bleeding. Carefully, very carefully, he carried the little rabbit back to camp, surprised at how easily he found his way now that he felt calm and purposeful.

He found the nurse, who washed out the wound and

bandaged it up. "It must have lost its mother somehow," she told him.

Nathan stayed there with the bunny almost all night, feeding it milk from the eye dropper the camp nurse had given him for that very purpose. Under his hand, the bunny stopped trembling and let Nathan pet its soft fur. Nathan didn't feel bad for himself at all anymore. Suddenly it seemed as though the day had gone perfectly.

"Just think," he whispered to the calm, still bunny, "if I hadn't lost my glasses, I wouldn't have gotten lost. If it hadn't started to rain, I wouldn't have stepped on that hornet's nest. If I hadn't run away from the hornets, I never would have found you, and you might have died all alone in that rotten old shed. But all those things did happen, and that sure was lucky. So that's what I'll call you: Lucky."

Nathan's mom dropped off another pair of glasses the next day, and things got a lot better. Nathan made new friends and brought them to see Lucky—who was getting a little stronger every day, but still wouldn't let anyone but Nathan pet him.

The rest of the week flew by. When it was time to go, Nathan went to say one last goodbye to Lucky, who the camp counselors planned to keep safe until his leg healed.

They then would release him back into the forest.

"Goodbye, and thanks for everything," Nathan said to Lucky, giving him a gentle hug. "Maybe I'll see you when I come back to camp next summer."

He was already looking forward to it.

DISCUSSION QUESTIONS:

Nathan has a day where bad thing after bad thing happens to him: first, he gets nothing but oatmeal for breakfast; then, he spills his oatmeal and gets a silly nickname; then, he drops his glasses into the lake, gets lost, and gets chased by a hive full of angry ground hornets. Have you ever had a day like that? Did things turn around for you in the way they did when Nathan rescued the rabbit?

Mirror, Mirror

THERE ONCE WAS A guinea pig named Princess. She lived in the Kingdom of the Guinea Pigs, a round and roly-poly Kingdom full of fat and furry guinea pigs.

Pretty much everything in the Kingdom was made of cardboard tubes and old newspapers and magazines. One day, as Princess was beginning to chew up a glossy magazine, she noticed that it was full of strange and beautiful humans wearing wonderful, colorful clothes. Each hairstyle was so creative—positively sculptural. Princess was inspired, and from that moment she devoted herself to becoming the most beautiful guinea pig in the whole Kingdom.

Using her fashion magazine as a guide, Princess worked hard to become beautiful. She rubbed red, black and green mud around her furry face and eyes, and spent hours—no, days—brushing thick white mud from the river into her hair so that she could mold it into a thousand shapes. She rubbed her body with flower petals. Sometimes she even made all the fur on her body stand straight up in little white points with pink ribbons tied to each one, which took her all day.

But no matter how hard she tried, she never felt pretty enough. She always worried that there were other guinea pigs even more beautiful than she. In due time she became Queen, and that's when things took a turn for the worse.

All day long, the Queen stood on her hind legs in front of the mirror. She barely ate, because the magazine taught her that to be beautiful she must be very, very skinny. The Queen quickly became a bony, mud-caked shadow of herself. She looked in the mirror all day long and was never satisfied with her reflection.

Her Highness passed a law making it a crime for any guinea pig to be more beautiful than she, and soon, the jails were full of poor little pigs who had been unfortunate enough to spark the Queen's jealousy. She set up Uglification Clinics where she would send pretty guinea pigs to have their ears clipped, their fur pulled out and their bodies rubbed with garbage. The more ugly everyone else looked, the more beautiful the Queen felt, but still, she never felt like she was beautiful enough.

The Kingdom became a very sad place. Most of her subjects began to leave the castle to set up a new village. Soon, the Kingdom was like a ghost town. But the Queen hardly noticed; she just spent even more time in front of the mirror. The guinea pig looking back at her was the only guinea pig she ever saw. She was terribly lonely and unhappy, but she couldn't admit it to herself.

"They just could not bear to compare their commonplace ugliness to my beauty," she murmured to herself. "They are all jealous of me. That's why they left!"

Days passed slowly into weeks and months. One day, having gone a bit crazy from loneliness and excessive mirror-gazing, she looked in the mirror and decided that the strange pig in the mirror was actually more beautiful than she was—a clear violation of the law! In a fit of rage, the Queen smeared the mirror with mud to make the mirror-pig uglier than she. But even then, the Queen thought she could still see some signs of beauty in the mirror-pig, so she covered the mirror with a

black rag, blotting out the guinea pig in the
mirror altogether.

It was then that the Queen finally realized that she
was truly alone. As she walked through empty cardboard
and newspaper streets, it occurred to her that finally,
she was the most beautiful guinea pig in the whole
Kingdom. Somehow, this didn't make her feel
very good.

The Kingdom slowly fell into ruin as the toilet paper
tubes and shredded newspaper rotted away in the rain.
The Queen was very lonely and, after a terrible downpour
that washed the colorful mud from her face and turned
her glossy-paper ball gown into a sodden mess, she quit.
She quit trying to be beautiful like the humans in the
magazine. For a long time, she stood out in the rain,
letting it wash her clean.

A few days later, a strange guinea pig quietly arrived
in the village her former subjects had built. She was
welcomed with kindness by friendly round pigs, who fed
her well enough to put some meat on her skinny frame.
Soon, she was as round and roly-poly as anyone, and she
felt a whole lot better.

She made friends, and in due time, fell in love and
got married. As she bundled her children into their

newspaper beds one night and looked into their shining eyes, she realized that for the first time, she understood what it really felt like to be beautiful.

DISCUSSION QUESTION:
Princess thinks that making herself look glamorous and thin will make her happy, but in the end, it doesn't – being herself and caring for others is what makes her feel beautiful. What makes you feel beautiful in that same way Princess does when she tucks in her children at bedtime?

The Emperor Who Was Afraid of Bunny Rabbits

A BOUT TWO HUNDRED YEARS ago, there lived a
powerful Emperor named Napoleon Bonaparte.
This is a story about him that is mostly true. I'll leave it
to you to figure out which parts of this story are made up
and which are not.[1]

Napoleon was just a little guy, not much taller than
a child, but he had very big dreams. Most of them were
about taking over other countries. Napoleon dreamed of
being the most powerful person in the whole world. He
started by taking over France and kept on going, building

1. Or, if you really want to know, check out *The Campaigns of Napoleon*, by David
Chandler (New York: The MacMillan Company, 1966) p. 593

an army that got bigger and bigger all the time. Soon, millions of men had been forced to put on blue uniforms and march all over Europe. They fought and fought and fought.

The Emperor did not see his soldiers as people so much as chessmen that he could move around a map of Europe. To him, the difficulties and dangers of war were all just a big game.

It was very important to Napoleon that everyone thought he was the best at everything. He was always showing off and trying to be better than everyone else, and he cheated at almost every game he played. His generals were so afraid of him that they pretended not to notice.

One day the Emperor decided he wanted to go rabbit hunting, but they couldn't find any rabbits for him to shoot. He got angrier and angrier. "*I want rabbits!*" he screamed. His most loyal general, Berthier, went off to see if he could find any.

He did find some, a whole bunch in fact, and so the Emperor went back to his palace to dress for the hunt. In his excitement the Emperor forgot his coat, and it was very cold outside. Standing in the empty field where he would soon be shooting rabbits, Napoleon noticed that one man was dressed in a warm and comfy-looking coat. "I want that coat," he demanded, and a few of his generals went over and ripped the coat off the poor man and threw him down into the snow. Napoleon put on the warm and comfy coat and felt much better. He didn't notice that the man was turning blue with cold. Even if he had noticed, he wouldn't have cared.

Finally, General Berthier arrived with a huge cart filled with hundreds of rabbits. Napoleon rubbed his hands together eagerly. He could hardly wait to start shooting. Berthier opened the cart and all the rabbits hippety-hopped down into the meadow in a big herd. But then something odd happened—or, rather, *didn't* happen.

The rabbits didn't run away. They just sat there twitching their rabbity noses and staring expectantly at the Emperor. Napoleon aimed his gun and yelled, "You better run, silly rabbits, because I am going to shoot every single one of you!" But they didn't run. They just stared at the Emperor even more intently, with a remarkably unafraid look in their little black eyes. And then, as the Emperor huffed and puffed with anger and surprise, the whole herd of rabbits started to hop...not *away* from the Emperor and his big gun, but right *at* him! Faster and faster they hopped in a huge, furry wave.

As it turned out, General Berthier had not been able to find any wild rabbits. Afraid of his Emperor's temper, he had bought several hundred *tame* rabbits for that day's hunt. And the man from whom Napoleon had taken the warm and comfy coat was actually the owner of all those rabbits. Naturally, when they saw Napoleon looking just like the nice man who fed them their carrots and lettuce every day, they hippety-hopped toward him, expecting their usual breakfast.

Napoleon didn't know this. All he knew was that he was being chased by several hundred rabbits with sharp, pointy teeth! He turned and ran with the rabbits hot on his heels, throwing his gun down as he went. Into his carriage he jumped, screaming for the driver to hurry up and drive. Some of the rabbits even managed to jump into the carriage with him. When Napoleon's generals heard him screaming in terror at this furry onslaught, they had to try very hard not to laugh.

Soon Napoleon, Emperor of France and half of Europe, was gone, his carriage fading into the distance with a rattle. Poor General Berthier knew he was going to be in really hot water with the Emperor, but for the moment, he had to figure out how on Earth he was going to gather up so many rabbits.

In the end, it wasn't hard at all. The rabbits, sensing that he was a good man, hippety-hopped on over, hoping that maybe he would be polite enough to give them their breakfast. Impulsively Berthier dropped to his knees and started petting and hugging them. They were soft and warm. It felt so good to bury his face in their fur.

In those moments, something inside that brave General shifted. He stood up, took off his sword belt, and threw his sword far into the woods. He took off his big plumed hat and kicked it like a ridiculous soccer ball. He ripped off his fancy gold medals and trudged through the snow to give them to the man whose coat Napoleon had stolen. And then he took a deep breath, picked up a beautiful grey bunny, tucked her under his arm, and walked away to start a new life.

Berthier had learned something important. He learned that just as rabbits are not furry little robots put on this earth to be hunted for our amusement, neither are human beings mere toys to be moved and sacrificed like chess pieces in some stupid game. And so he walked away.

As it was, the Napoleonic Wars led to the deaths of more than three million people. But if the Emperor had been braver—if he had stopped to pet those bunnies instead of running away from them—maybe he would have been awakened to the value of life, just like General Berthier was. Maybe he would have told his enormous army to put down their guns forever.

DISCUSSION QUESTION:

Berthier knelt and petted the bunnies, and this reminded him of the value of all kinds of life and the craziness of war. How would you tell the end of this story if Napoleon had done the same?

The Broken Flute

B EING HURT OR SICK is never fun, and being stuck in a hospital room can be scary. In many hospitals, there are ministers whose job is simply to visit with people: sitting with them, sometimes holding their hands, listening—just being there, so they won't feel so scared or alone. A minister who works in a hospital is called a chaplain.

Emily was a warm and grandmotherly kind of person who worked as a volunteer chaplain in a large hospital. She had rich brown hair and big circular plastic-rimmed glasses that made her eyes look even bigger and kinder than they already were. Her husband had passed away years before, and since then, she had comforted thousands of patients right there in the same hospital where her husband had once been a patient.

One of Emily's favorite things to do was to play the recorder. She had lots of recorders: some were made of wood and some were made of metal; some played high tones and others played lower; some had crystal-clear sound and others had softer, more soothing tones. She loved them all, but she did have one special favorite.

Her favorite recorder was made of a beautiful dark wood, which was faded and pale from where her fingers had held it over the years. It made the clearest, purest, most beautiful music of all her recorders, and when she played it in the hospital, the music echoed far and wide. She carried the recorder with her everywhere she went.

When she went on a backpacking trip, Emily carried her favorite recorder in her pocket like she always did. But on the second night of her trip, she accidentally sat on it! She reached into her pocket desperately, hoping against hope that it would be okay…but it wasn't. Her favorite recorder had a terrible crack in it. She was so sad.

But she kept the broken recorder. When she got back from her trip, she tried everything she could think of to fix it. Nothing worked. When Emily blew into it, no sound came out at all except the sound of her breath.

All her friends said, "Come on, Emily, can't you see it's ruined? You might as well just throw it away." But she kept it anyway. She continued to carry it around with her even though it couldn't make music anymore.

One day she was visiting with a patient who also played flutes and recorders. He even made his own! Emily nervously said, "I know you aren't feeling very well these days, but maybe you can help me." She pulled out the broken recorder. "I was so stupid. I accidentally sat on the poor thing and broke it. Is there anything you can think of that might fix it? It's very special to me."

He examined it. "Well, it is a bad crack…let's see what we can do." They sat side by side on the edge of his bed as he patiently worked on the instrument. When they were through, she held the recorder to her lips eagerly, ready for the music to flow.

Nothing happened. The silence was deafening. Emily's eyes filled with disappointed tears. "Thanks anyhow," she said to the patient, who looked apologetically into her eyes and shrugged, then lay back in his bed for a rest.

After that, Emily still carried that recorder around with her everywhere she went. Sometimes she felt compelled to pull it out and put it to her lips, just in case some magic might have happened to bring the instrument back to life. And one day, when she blew into that recorder, out came the most beautiful, quiet, warm, full tone she had ever heard!

The music that came out of that miraculous old recorder had changed. Its voice was quieter now. It had mellowed from the clear, ringing voice of its youth to a sound like soft words or a gentle lullaby. Emily soon realized that this new sound suited the hospital perfectly.

One day, as she did her rounds, she was surprised to see that the old musician who had helped her fix the recorder was back in the hospital again. He was very sick.

"I'm so glad to see you again!" Emily said. " I mean, I'm sad that you're sick, but the most amazing thing has happened! My recorder works again. Better than ever."

The old man smiled and said, "Let me see." Emily drew the instrument out of her pocket and handed it to him. He ran his sensitive, wrinkled hands all over the wood, tracing the scar where it had been broken. His eyes smiled. "We couldn't heal this break on our own, could we?" he went on. "But I see now what happened. The seasons changed."

"What do changing seasons have to do with it?" Emily asked.

"As the wood got wetter and drier and warmer and

cooler with time, it expanded. The gradual swelling mended the crack. And you were patient, loyal and loving enough to let that happen on its own."

Looking at her with his tired brown eyes, he handed the recorder back to Emily. He asked in a weary but satisfied voice, "Will you play for me?"

With grateful tears welling up in her eyes, she began to play, and the music that came from her favorite flute was soft and pure and beautiful. As the music filled that cold room to overflowing, even the busiest nurses passing by the doorway outside paused to listen. When she finished her song, he sighed contentedly.

"Sometimes, Emily, it's the broken instruments that have the best sound," he said to her. And she knew he was right.

DISCUSSION QUESTIONS:
Music can help us feel better during hard times. What makes you feel better when life is tough?

A Church Mouse Christmas

'T WAS THE NIGHT BEFORE Christmas, and as was their tradition, the Greynose family of church mice was hard at work making the church absolutely perfect for Christmas services.

Every speck of dust and every single crumb was cleaned away, no matter how small. Even the littlest mice helped out, sliding head-first down through the organ pipes like miniature dust mops to ensure that the organ would sound its best.

In the middle of their preparations, the mice heard a terribly sad mewing sound from outside the church doors. Old Moses Greynose, the Mayor of the mice, crept quietly out to see what was the matter.

There, curled up on the rainy church steps, was a soggy, sick-looking cat. She was too weak to stand. All she could do was lie there and meow mournfully. Moses, like all mice, was terrified of cats, and he was about to go back inside when her sad eyes met his. He knew he couldn't leave her outside in the cold rain.

Moses went inside to get help from the other mice. Of course, none of them would help. "A cat? We can't have a cat in here! Don't you remember what happened to Uncle Morty?" chided Mitchell.

Moses and his wife Millie tried to persuade the other mice to help out, but they were too afraid. Finally, they agreed to have a look at the cat for themselves—from a safe distance, of course. And sure enough, when the Greynoses saw that poor cat lying helplessly in a cold puddle, they just couldn't leave her out there.

It took every single able-bodied mouse to move the cat into the church. They made a bed in the warm, dark organ loft, where none of the humans ever went. Later, as the church filled with Christmas songs and the organ boomed, the sick cat was able to rest comfortably despite a raging fever. And sometime that night, as the humans lit their candles in the dark sanctuary, a single scruffy kitten was born.

Millie and Moses discovered the new kitten when they brought some warm milk up to its mother—who, even after a night's rest, hadn't not gotten any better. Refusing the milk, the mother cat begged them with hot, wet eyes: *Please, please take care of my kitten.* The two Greynoses nodded their heads in agreement, and the poor cat closed her eyes for the last time.

After the humans left, the church mice gathered in the organ loft for an emergency meeting. They were divided on what to do next. Many of the mice wanted to get rid of the kitten. "To bring a sick cat in from the rain is bad enough—but to raise a kitten into a vicious cat?! Impossible!" shouted Marla, whose best friend had been chased and almost eaten by a cat. Others argued that the kitten was too helpless to survive if they were to put it outside. "I know cats eat mice," said Mason, the mayor's eldest son, "but it's helpless, and if we don't take care of it, no one will."

Then, suddenly, as the argument raged back and forth, the little pink kitten whimpered, stretched, and opened its eyes for the first time. That was the end of the argument. Only a mouse with a heart of stone could look into those soft eyes and remain unmoved.

All the mice pitched in to nurse that kitten through its

first weeks, feeding it half-and-half from the tiny plastic containers the humans sometimes used. The little cat, that they named Christmas, grew into a fine young feline. As his fur grew in, the mice saw that their little Christmas even had a grey patch on his nose just like theirs! It beautifully complemented his shiny black body. And so he was known as Christmas Greynose, the biggest of the church mice.

Christmas was too big to slide down the organ pipes with the other mice, but he could do lots of things the other mice couldn't. He made sure that no other cats less civilized than he tried to eat the mice, and he scared away the rats that raided the church every now and then. The other mice could only carry tiny crumbs, but Christmas could carry whole wedges of delicious cheese in his jaws, which he enjoyed just as much as the rest of his family.

The humans *loved* Christmas the cat, especially when he purred, walking soft-furred figure eights around their legs, hypnotizing them with his beautiful blue eyes. They'd say, "Oh, what a darling cat!" and give him all sorts of wonderful treats right off their plates—treats he would immediately bring back to share with his adoptive family.

And so a whole year passed and Christmas Eve came

again. The mice turned a bit of leftover greenery into a tree two towering feet high. They could reach the higher branches easily when Christmas Greynose let them climb onto his back, but they let their feline friend have the biggest honor: that of stretching up to place a clean white piece of popcorn on top like a star.

DISCUSSION QUESTION:

The helplessness of the kitten gives the Graynose family the courage to adopt him. Share about a time when you were afraid and found the courage to be kind or helpful.

Robots in Love

ONCE UPON A TIME, there was a rather insignificant planet that orbited a rather average star. On that planet was a city called Toolbox. There were no human beings there, and no animals or birds, but the city of Toolbox was far from empty. Thousands upon thousands of robots lived there.

There were two kinds of robots in Toolbox. Some of the robots had large, heavy, square heads and the others had long, narrow, cone-shaped heads. Nobody could remember who had built these robots, or why or where the builders had gone. Whoever had built them had expertly devised a system of lights that allowed them to visualize their world through their consoles, as Toolbox was a dark place where no moon or sun ever shone.

Almost all of the laws in the city had to do with which kind of robot you were. Square-headed robots, called Squares, and the cone-headed robots, called Cones, never had anything to do with one another. Every room and every part of the city was clearly labeled with a square or a cone, and only that kind of robot was allowed inside. When robots had to go from place to place, they rode on moving sidewalks that were also clearly labeled so that the two kinds of robots always remained separate from one another.

One night, all the power went out in the city of Toolbox. The sidewalks ground to a halt, the lights went out, and the robots had to run on their emergency batteries, which meant that they pretty much had to just stand around and wait for the power to come back on.

It so happened that on this particular day, at the particular moment when the power went out, two robots were riding the moving sidewalk in opposite directions. One was a Square named 247XG and the other was a Cone named XK196. When the power went out, the sidewalk stopped, leaving them standing in the dark right across one another on the broken sidewalk.

The two robots stood very still to conserve their reserve

batteries. They stood there for a long time, for several days in fact, which isn't really a big problem for robots since they don't have to eat or go to the bathroom. As long as their power reserves hold out, they can amuse themselves by playing computer games in their heads. But even for robots, it was a long time to be standing alone in the dark.

Finally, on day 7 or 8, Square 247XG spoke. "Can you hear me over there?"

"Yep," Cone XK196 replied after a pause.

Those were pretty ordinary words, considering they were the first words a Square had ever said to a Cone in the whole long history of Toolbox City.

"How's it goin' over there?" Square 247XG went on, boldly.

"Oh, pretty good, considering. A little boring, but such is life, right?" replied Cone XK196.

"I hear you."

And that was pretty much that for their first conversation.

After several more days of standing there in the dark waiting for the power to come back on, their boredom overcame them and they started to talk. And talk. And talk. Square 247XG and Cone XK196 had never talked so much in their whole shelf lives! It turned out they had a lot in common. 247XG always had something thought-provoking to say and XK196 was always quick with a joke. "What's the difference between a transverse heat shield and a regulating dongle?" XK196 would ask. "Seven!" The LAUGHTER buttons on their consoles would light up brilliantly. "I never get tired of that one," 247XG would chuckle.

Over the next couple weeks, this forbidden friendship continued. By the time the power came back on, the two robots were the very best of friends.

When the sidewalks started rolling again, Cone and Square exchanged r-mail addresses and made arrangements to meet up again, but it was hard, since there were hardly any places where Squares and Cones could even be within shouting distance of one another. They took to riding around on the moving sidewalks all day long because that was the only way they could be close together: one riding along just a few feet from the other, in parallel.

But the other robots started to talk.

"Cones and Squares riding moving sidewalks together? Disgusting!"

"R-mailing one another at all hours? Hideous! Intolerable!"

And so the robot police of Toolbox demanded they stop seeing one another. If they insisted on continuing with this unprecedented friendship, they would both be sent to the recycling center for crushing. But 247XG and XK196 refused. These two robots had come to care for and love one another very deeply and they weren't going to back down for anyone. So they demanded a trial where all the robots would come to the City Center to hear their case.

Such a thing had never happened before, but eventually, the robot police agreed to it. The whole city was in an uproar, and a trial might be just the thing to draw all this insanity to a close.

On the day of the great trial, many thousands of robots crammed into the big central square to hear the case. The Chief Robot boomed, "You have been charged with an illegal, immoral and generally yucky friendship with a robot with the wrong head-shape. How do you plead: guilty or not guilty?"

"Your honor," replied the Cone, "I love 247XG and it loves me, same head-shape or no, and there is nothing you can do about it."

"Is this true?" the Chief Robot thundered at the Square.

After a pause, the Square, who was a robot of few words, answered, "Yup."

"Then I have no choice but to sentence you both to

be sent to the recycling center to be crushed into small metal cubes!" And the Chief Robot's henchrobots began to advance toward 247XG and XK196.

"Not so fast," said the Square, pushing a little button it had spent the last couple of months building into its arm. Suddenly everything went black as all the power in Toolbox went out.

Mayhem erupted. Tens of thousands of robots banged into one another and flailed in the pitch dark. As time passed and the lights and power did not come back on, however, the robots, who were running on emergency power, had to give it up. Eventually, they all stood still, waiting in the darkness.

Square, standing side by side with Cone, kept the power off for a good long time—for years, in fact. And a funny, but entirely predictable thing happened: the robots started to talk to one another, just as Cone and Square had so long ago. In the darkness, there was no way to know what head-shape anyone had, and soon, new inter-model friendships were popping up all over the place. Square waited another five or ten years for good measure, and then pressed his little button again. All at once, the lights of Toolbox flickered to life.

The robots found themselves console-to-console with

their new friends—many of whom had different head-shapes. All at once, they realized how silly they had been for all those centuries. Needless to say, the trial was over, and nobody was going to get crushed in the recycler.

And so all the robots went home to plug into their battery chargers like always, but things were different after that. Many robot historians point to the Great Square and Cone Trial as the moment when Toolbox City began its golden age.

DISCUSSION QUESTIONS:

According to the laws of Toolbox, Squares and Cones are not allowed to talk to each other. Although it seems hard to believe, many cultures throughout history have had rules like these, where people who are different from each other are not supposed to be friends. What do you think of rules like these?

The other residents of Toolbox gossip about the forbidden friendship between Cone XK196 and Square 247XG. Do people gossip in your world?

The Medicine Tree

SINCE LONG, LONG AGO, when the first of the mighty trees was just a seedling, the animals who lived in the Great Wood have possessed a powerful Medicine. It was made out of many different ingredients, and all the animals had to work together to make it.

Each animal species had a special role in gathering the Medicine's many parts from the forest floor, the plants, the stream, the sky, and the overarching canopy. They all knew the recipe and they all understood how the Medicine was made. Deer were in charge of sweet grass; otters brought the brown clay; and families of mice carried back small leaves full of fresh rainwater.

This Medicine, potent as it was, couldn't heal everything. Deer and jaguar, tree toad and tree sloth, ground squirrel and bear all still died of old age, injury or illness. Still, by and large, the medicine did help keep the animals healthy and happy in the Great Wood that was their home.

Most of the animals kept a little bit of Medicine in the nests and burrows and lily pads and fallen logs where they lived. But one year, a lightning strike started a huge forest fire. As the animals worked to fight the fire and to take care of one another, they decided that the safest place for the Medicine was the underground burrows of the ground squirrels. Even after the fire died out, the ground squirrels kept the Medicine out of harm's way. The squirrels also came to be charged with making more Medicine when it was needed.

In time, the ground squirrels were the only creatures in the Great Wood who remembered how to make the Medicine. When a marmot got its leg snapped in a trap, when a nest full of baby mice came down with fever, or when a raccoon had an ingrown toenail, they went to the ground squirrels for some Medicine.

In gratitude for the ground squirrels' help, the other animals often brought gifts of food as a way of saying thank you. Before long, the ground squirrels had grown fat from these offerings.

At the beginning of every month, the Chief Ground Squirrel climbed up onto a high tree branch. In a loud, proud voice, he announced to each animal family its role in gathering ingredients for the Medicine from the Great Wood. The ground squirrels didn't go out and fetch anything; they just gave orders in their chattering voices.

As more years passed, the ground squirrels started to get greedy. They started to believe that although they needed the help of all the other animals to make the Medicine, it really belonged to them. And they believed that because of this, they were the most powerful and wise of the animals of the Great Wood.

One day, a friendly little pond frog named José came to the ground squirrels for help. He had a terrible cold; his nose was completely stuffed and his throat was so sore that he couldn't even croak! He feebly hopped over to the ground squirrels' Waiting Room and asked for some Medicine.

"Where is our gift?" the squirrels demanded. "No gift, no Medicine."

José was so sick and weak that he could not collect any food, not even to feed himself, so he had no gift to

give. The squirrels turned up their twitching noses and refused to give him any Medicine. José hopped sadly away and was never heard from again.

After this, the squirrels always demanded gifts, which they now called "payment." No matter how sick or hurt they were, animals who couldn't pay were turned away. Meanwhile, the squirrels got fatter and fatter. Their underground burrows overflowed with all the treasures of the forest. They even paid some bigger, more ferocious animals to guard their burrows and to scare any animal who started to speak out against them.

Prices for Medicine kept going up until almost none of the animals could afford what had once been free to all. The animals got angrier and angrier as their sick friends and children and elders tried to get Medicine and were turned away.

On the last night of the full moon, many of the animals got together for a secret meeting. Bluebirds, newts, brook trout, deer and even bobcats were there, along with many other animals. They decided that Raven, the most clever of all the birds, should get the recipe for the Medicine back from the ground squirrels. Once the recipe for the Medicine was in their possession again, they could take care of one another just as they once had.

Raven waited until the beginning of the next month, when the Medicine was almost gone and the Chief Squirrel had summoned all the creatures of the Great Wood to the tree to be assigned their work for the month. He hid in the very topmost branches of the tree, high above the Chief Squirrel, until the Chief held up the ingredient list and cleared his throat importantly. Silent as an arrow, Raven swooped down and snatched the Medicine recipe right out of the squirrel's paws. The squirrels and their thugs went crazy, but none of them could catch Raven, who flew so fast and hid so well in every dark shadow.

The next morning, all the animals woke up to a wonderful surprise. Raven had stayed up all night carving the Medicine recipe into the bark of a giant redwood tree! Once again, the recipe was available to all. All the animals—except for the squirrels, who were busy moping and plotting revenge down in their burrows—gathered around and laughed and danced and celebrated for the rest of the day. The morning after that, they all went out and collected the ingredients they needed, which they then cut and chopped and squished and powdered until they had a wonderful new batch of Medicine.

From that day forth, the giant carved redwood was known as the Medicine Tree. All the sick animals went there for help. They all worked together to make sure there was always enough Medicine to go around. In and around the Medicine Tree, the animals made beds of straw or snug, dry healing burrows for any sick animal who might need one. For the creatures that lived in water, there were healing puddles; healing nests were constructed for those who lived in nests.

At first, the squirrels would have nothing to do with the Medicine tree. They acted as though they had been robbed. But a few months later one of the newest, cutest, and fuzziest baby ground squirrels accidentally ate a poisonous berry and got very sick indeed. In desperation, the squirrels took the baby to the Medicine Tree, sure that they would be turned away.

Guiltily, with bowed heads, they approached the Tree. But Raven and the other animals took the little squirrel in without a word. They gently laid her on a soft bed made of grass and leaves. Raven dropped some of the Medicine from his beak into the baby's mouth. By now, all the squirrels were crying: from relief, of course, but also because they realized all the hurt their selfishness and greed had caused.

Wendy the black bear lumbered up to Chief Squirrel and laid her big paw gently on his back. "This Medicine belongs to all of us, even you," she said to him softly. "Everyone who ever needs Medicine shall have some."

The squirrels tried to say how sorry they were for having denied the Medicine to any of member of the animal family of the Great Wood, but they couldn't find the words.

"We forgive you," Wendy said gently. "Welcome back."

DISCUSSION QUESTIONS:

The ground squirrels became greedy when they saw that the other animals would bring them gifts of food in order to get Medicine. Have you ever seen others become greedy? Have you ever felt greedy yourself? What happened when greed became a driving force for you or for someone else?

The Seagull and the Garbage Dump

A LTHOUGH MAX WAS EVERY inch a seagull, with beautiful white feathers, strong wings and a curved beak made for catching fish, he had never so much as heard of the ocean.

Max had always lived in a giant garbage dump on the edge of town. He had learned to soar over vast hills of rotting vegetables and old furniture. His curved beak had never tasted fish aside from what the humans threw in their trash—and by the time that got to the dump, it was hardly ever good enough to eat.

Still, life was pretty good for Max. He had plenty of

friends. And since the garbage dump was the only world he had ever known, he didn't think it was all that bad.

He grew up smart and resourceful like all the seagulls did in the dump. But in some ways, he wasn't like the other birds. He told great jokes and he was deeply kind.

The dump was a dangerous place. Life was hard and short. The worst danger was from all the traps and poisoned food left out by the humans who ran the dump. But Max's inborn kindness only deepened in the harsh world of garbage. He saw many of his friends get sick, lose feet and even die, but instead of hardening him, these difficulties just made his heart grow even bigger and gentler. Max was the only bird who was loved by the rats and gulls alike.

But for all the good things in Max's life (he especially loved Thursdays, when the trucks came to dump tons of fresh garbage), he always felt like something was missing. He never felt quite at home in the dump, and yet he couldn't imagine a world outside of it.

But one day, as Max was sunning himself on the great mound in the middle of the dump, a strange smell wafted by. It was like nothing he had ever smelled before: fresh, clean...and salty. His feathers shivered in recognition. Of what? He didn't know.

Max threw himself into the air and glided back and forth, trying to stay in the scent, trying not to lose it, whatever it was. Without realizing it, he flew much farther than he had ever flown before. He flew and flew and flew, hardly noticing as the garbage dump vanished behind him.

A good while later, the wonderful scent began to get much stronger. Max opened his eyes wide in wonder as a powerful, fresh wind tickled his feathers. How could the air be so soft and sweet? And then, as he flew past one last rise in the earth, before him lay an incredible vista: the setting sun, soft white sand and miles and miles of waves. Birds he had never seen before danced above the surface of the undulating water. His heart beat hard with a feeling he had never felt before, but later called *joy*.

Max the Seagull had found his way to the ocean.

He made friends at the oceanside just as he had at the dump, which was a good thing, because he quickly discovered he had a lot to learn about being a seagull. He learned how to ride the winds, dive for fish and charm tourists into throwing him tasty breadcrumbs. In the dump, he had looked and sounded like a seagull, but he couldn't be the true seagull he was born to be until he found his way to the ocean.

But something was still missing in Max's almost perfect

life. One evening, as he sat on a post watching a pod of dolphins swim by, he realized what it was. His friends back in the dump had no idea all of this existed!

The next morning, Max flew back toward the garbage dump, guided by a much different smell than the one that had led him to the sea. He landed on top of the great stinking mound and was quickly surrounded by old friends.

"Where on Earth have you been?!" they squawked.

"Well, you're not going to believe it, but I swear, it's all true…" he began, and then he told them.

The other gulls were very confused. Some of them

didn't believe him. Some thought he was crazy and others were even angry, as if he were trying to trick them. None of them seemed willing to even imagine that there might be another world, a better world beyond the borders they had always known. Plus, Max was *different* now, and this made them uncomfortable.

Still, everyone was so happy to see him. They presented him with their choicest scraps of trash and invited him to stay the night before flying back to the strange new place he was now calling home.

In the darkness that night, a young gull was caught in a terrible trap. She was in a lot of pain and would probably not make it to morning. Max sat beside her and stroked her feathers with his gentle beak. To keep her mind off the pain, he told her all about the ocean and about what seagull life can really be like. As her eyes slowly faded, the crowd of gulls who had gathered to listen were silent and thoughtful.

The next morning, Max said goodbye and lifted off to return to the ocean. Three other gulls decided to make the trip with him, and although it was scary at first, they were glad they took this journey. After that, Max continued to spend a lot of his time at the seashore, and hard times sometimes found him there just like they had at the dump.

But he had changed for good. He was a seagull now, all the way through. He had found the ocean. And for the rest of his life, he flew back and forth between the ocean and the dump, helping other birds find their way.

DISCUSSION QUESTIONS:

The other seagulls are afraid to leave the dump to follow Max to the ocean, despite all the wonderful things he tells them about it. In your world, do people sometimes seem afraid of change—even good change?

The Wonders of Duct Tape

THERE ONCE WAS A small village on an island far out in the great blue sea. The people had been living there for generations, catching fish and farming small plots of land that extended right to the edges of the sharp cliffs that overlooked the ocean.

Because they lived so far away from the mainland, the people of the island had to take care of themselves. Most of their tools and houses had been around for a very long time. Whenever anything broke, they would call Mr. Tinker, an old man who could fix almost anything.

One day, an unfamiliar sailboat pulled into the harbor. The man who owned the ship came ashore with boxes and crates full of all kinds of wonderful things. He set up a tent on the beach and opened shop with a big banner overhead that read:

Buy More! Pay Less!

The things he sold—the shovels, axes, plows, cooking pots and radios—were all super cheap. The people of the island went a little crazy and bought almost everything, whether they needed it or not, because it seemed like such a good deal.

They quickly began to realize, however, that all that stuff was cheap for a reason: it was terrible. Everything they bought broke almost the first time they tried to use it. Soon, a long line of angry islanders were clamoring for their money back.

The salesman reassuringly held out his hands to the crowd. "Relax, my friends. Relax. Things break: that's life. And here, just look—I have the answer to all your problems." He lifted a sticky, shiny grey cylinder over his head like a holy relic.

It was a roll of duct tape.

The man showed the villagers how duct tape could "fix" almost anything. He showed them how, with enough duct tape, they could close up holes in the ceiling, fix broken bicycle frames or fishing rods, broken spoons, or even the old red tractor whose parts had become so rusty that they kept falling off at inopportune times. And then, he packed up his tent and sailed away with his pockets full of money.

Amazed, the people bought every single roll of duct tape they could. They all went around the village wrapping it around everything that was broken or looked like it might break. People were even seen holding their rolls of duct tape reverently above their heads as though they were sacred treasures.

Nobody came to Mr. Tinker anymore when they needed something mended. Why invest in his services when they could just slap on some duct tape? Meanwhile, Mr. Tinker kept his shop as neat and tidy as ever. His family was the only one on the whole island who didn't own any of the magic tape. It just didn't interest them.

In the evenings, Tinker sat out on his porch with his young daughters on his lap, reading brightly colored brochures. He watched as his village became more and more shiny and "duct tape-grey" as one thing after another broke down, as things do without proper care and maintenance.

"What are you reading, Mr. Tinker?" asked his wife.

"Just some travel brochures, Mrs. Tinker, dearest one. I'm trying to decide where we should go on our vacation. What do you think? London? Paris? I hear Greece is wonderful this time of year."

Well, Mrs. Tinker loved Mr. Tinker very much, but she wondered how he could even think about vacations at such a time. "Are you crazy?" she asked him gently. "You haven't had any work for weeks now! We're almost out of food."

"Just wait, my dear, just wait," he replied calmly. "What do you think about Tokyo?"

Then, just as the sun began to set, a terrible storm rose up and slashed down upon the island. It brought endless sheets of rain and howling winds. The storm lasted for three long days and nights. And what do you suppose the villagers saw when they finally came out and looked around their town?

Almost everything they owned had collapsed into a sticky, gross, shapeless heap of grey gook. The rainwater had dissolved the sticky glue on the back of the tape, and everything the islanders had "fixed" with their hundreds of rolls of duct tape—every leaky roof, every broken plow and fishing pole—all of these things had fallen apart once more. They had never really been fixed at all, only held together temporarily.

Mr. Tinker, standing on his porch, smiled and nodded his head. He put on his apron and turned the sign on his door to the side that read "Open" and in less than half an hour, an enormous line of customers had gathered outside his shop. Gingerly, they held all manner of broken things, which were now covered in sticky goo.

"What do you think, kids?" Mr. Tinker asked while he worked. "Disney World looks like a lot of fun." Eyeing the growing line of customers, he went on. "Perhaps we can do Disney World *and* Paris. I hear Paris is lovely in the springtime."

DISCUSSION QUESTIONS:

Why might it be better to build finer things and fix them when they break than to patch poorly made things with duct tape—or, as we tend to do in our modern world, throw them out and buy more poorly made things?

Mr. Tinker's family worries when villagers stop bringing him their things to fix, but Mr. Tinker doesn't seem worried. Why?

Do you have something precious or beautiful that you would do anything to fix if it broke?

Too Much of a Good Thing

O NCE UPON A TIME, when the world was young, there was a great forest. The trees grew so tall and close together that the forest floor was always very dark. In that dark place, there lived many animals: squirrels, picas, skunks, possums and near-sighted moles. The animals never went hungry, even in that dim world where almost nothing grew, for way up high in the canopy grew the most amazing berries.

The berries grew at the very top of the very tallest tree, where the Sun shone close enough to touch. Every night, the berries fell whenever the West Wind blew. They dropped like soft rain on the dark ground below, and the animals ate to their heart's content.

Raven, who was between adventures, happened to fly over the great forest. He was tired from flying and from the beat of the warm sun on his shiny black wings. So he landed on the highest branch of the tallest tree to take a rest. His bright eyes, which were keen enough to count a single line of ants from the top of the world's tallest mountain, noticed the plump red berries almost immediately.

Now, he might not look like it—he is only about two feet long from the tip of his beak tip to the end of his tail feathers—but that Raven can *eat*. By nightfall, he had gobbled down pretty much every tree berry he could find. When the West Wind started to blow, the animals of the forest waited in vain for the rain of berries to begin.

Not a single berry fell. Nothing fell at all except a seed or two that Raven burped out after finishing his meal high above them.

After a few hungry days, the animals of the ground sent a delegation of squirrels up to the canopy to see what was going on. On the very top of the tallest tree they found Raven, his greedy beak stained with berry-juice.

"Dear Raven," called the squirrels, "You are new here and so probably don't know it, but we all depend on those berries you've just gobbled up. Help yourself, oh mighty one, but please leave some for the rest of us!"

Raven looked at them blandly. "Silly squirrels, don't you know who I am? I am Raven, Stealer of the Sun, Trickster of the Moon. The whole world sings of my adventures. Surely I, being so much more important than you, am entitled to eat as many of these delicious berries as I please!"

"But Raven, we will starve!" said one squirrel.

Raven sighed. "Well, I'm not a monster, you know. Here is what I will do. I, generous Raven, will eat my fill of berries. But never fear! When I am full, I will let the extra berries fall to you."

"You will let the food we need to survive...*trickle down* to us?" asked another squirrel. His brothers and sisters chattered nervously, their tails shaking with concern.

"Yes! In effect, the berries will *trickle down*," Raven replied. "I *do* like the sound of that. Oh, don't worry, my dear squirrels! There'll be plenty. This is the way of the world." And with that, he turned away, tucked his beak under one wing, and settled down for a nap.

In the end, the dejected delegation had no choice but to turn tail and go back down to tell the rest of the animals what Raven had said.

The next few weeks were hungry ones. Raven tried to

keep his promise, but the more Raven ate, the more his stomach stretched; the more his stomach stretched, the more room it had for berries! Soon, Raven's black body didn't look Raven-like at all. From a distance he looked more like a bowling ball with wings. The slender branches upon which Raven perched drooped more and more each day under the fat bird's growing weight.

One morning Raven saw the most beautiful, scrumptious, juicy, delectable berry he had ever seen! He was already so stuffed he could barely move, but it looked too good to pass up. "Just. One. More. Berry," he groaned.

Snap! Crack! went the branch, and suddenly Raven was falling as fast as only a feathery bowling ball can fall. He flapped his wings desperately, to no avail. Raven fell and fell and fell, squawking *"Heeeeeellllllpp meeeeeee!"* all the way down. He fell from such a great height that once they heard him start to fall, the animals of the forest had plenty of time to come out of their holes, burrows and nests to watch.

After what seemed like a very long time to the animals (and much too short a time to Raven), he hit the ground like a cannonball. The impact forced the loudest, longest burp in the whole long history of the world out of his overstuffed body. This burp was so powerful that all the berries Raven had stuffed down his gullet—and there were hundreds of them—burst out of him like candy from an exploding piñata.

The berries flew into the air and fell to the ground like rain. And when they hit the ground, something extraordinary happened. These berries, having been 'planted' inside of Raven, had absorbed some of his magic. (Remember, Raven may be a fool, but he is a magical fool.)

The now-magical and still-delicious berries almost immediately took root and began to grow into mighty bushes. The berries that sprouted from these bushes were still red, but were accompanied by strange black flowers every bit as black and ragged as Raven's own feathers.

"Hurrah!" cried the squirrels and possums and picas and skunks.

"Yes, indeed, most definitely, hurrah," croaked Raven weakly as he climbed to his feet, his stomach empty once again. "Hurrah for Raven, Stealer of the Sun, Charmer of the Moon…and Bringer of Berries? Hurrah for me?"

The animals saw how embarrassed Raven was, and promised they would never tell anyone the real story of how it had all come to pass.

Raven, having lost both his bowling-ball belly and his appetite for berries, flew away in search of new adventures. And wherever he went, his version of the story became more and more outlandish. He painted himself as the great hero who generously fed a forest full of creatures with all the berries it could eat. The animals of the forest never contradicted him. They just smiled and nibbled knowingly on their forest's abundant bounty.

DISCUSSION QUESTIONS:

In the end, Raven literally explodes from taking more than his fair share! Have you ever taken more than your share? What ended up happening?

The Field:
An Easter Story[1]

L ITTLE DOROTHEE SAT ON the front porch swing every afternoon, reading a book or coloring while waiting for her dad to come home from work. When she heard the sound of his beat-up old car turning onto their gravel driveway from the road, she jumped to her feet, leapt off the porch and waited to give him a big hug as soon as he got out of the car. She carried his briefcase into the house for him, and they shared an afternoon snack: fresh peaches from the tree in their backyard when they were ripe, and graham crackers and milk when they weren't.

---

1. This story was inspired by my friend Dorothee Hahn, who saw such a field as a young girl in Germany.

Father was a professor at the university, and he was
always busy, but he made time for Dorothee no matter
how busy he got until he started writing a new book. A big
book. Super thick, like a phone book. He said it was the
book he'd always wanted to write.

His study filled up with papers and books, and he
seemed to spend every spare moment in there working,
his eyes blinking tiredly in the blue light of the computer
screen. He didn't have time for snacks anymore, and often
worked until long after Dorothee's bedtime. Some days,
he even worked straight through dinner—always on that
stupid old book.

Dorothee was sad. She missed her father so much, but
he didn't even seem to notice her anymore. Sometimes
she sat out on the porch waiting for him for hours, and
her mother had to bring her dinner out to her because
she refused to leave her post. Finally, when Dorothee fell
asleep, her mother would carry her to bed.

She tried everything she could think of to get her
dad's attention. Watercolor paintings were painted and
presented to him while he pored over research books
at his desk. Jokes were made up and told to him while
he reviewed his writing for the day. But he'd just say,
"Thanks, honey!" or "Very nice, dear," without even

looking up. Then, he'd shoo her out of the office, saying something like, "Run along now, Dorothee, I've just got to finish this chapter, okay?"

"Everything was great before that stupid book came along," she told her pet bunny, Hubert, one day when her father was still at work and her mother was making dinner. "Now he doesn't even care about me at all." As she felt her anger growing, she knew she had to do something with all those big feelings.

Dorothee found herself sneaking into her father's study. She pulled out her magic markers and colored all over his papers and notes and even inside some of his books.

Her dad and her mom were going to be furious, but she didn't care. Maybe if she ruined his book, maybe *then* he would notice her. She sat right there in the mess she'd made and waited for her father to get home.

When he came into his office, he took one look around and his face got very red. He took a deep breath, took off his glasses and rubbed his eyes. Dorothee had never seen him look so old. "Go to your room," he said quietly.

As she lay in bed feeling terrible, she could hear the voices of her mother and father in their room, but she couldn't make out what they were saying. Late at night, she finally fell asleep. It seemed she had only been asleep for a few seconds when she felt her father's hand on her arm, shaking her awake.

"Get dressed, and come with me...quietly," he whispered. Dorothee stumbled into her clothes and down the stairs, terrified that she was in for the worst punishment ever.

Her father hurried her out to the car. It wasn't even dawn yet and the night was cold and wet. A thin powder of frost covered everything like a blanket.

They didn't talk as they drove. After a while her father turned off the main road onto an old farm road. He drove to the top of a big hill, pulled over, and turned off the car. They got out and he spread a big blanket on the ground. He pulled out a big thermos of hot chocolate, a giant loaf of fresh French bread and some apples and cheese.

Dorothee was just working up the courage to ask when her punishment was going to begin when a sliver of sun rose over the valley as if reeled up by a gigantic fishing pole. As dawn light blazed across the big meadow below them, Dorothee gasped in surprise.

Beneath them, covering the whole valley floor, were

hundreds and hundreds of rabbits. Throngs of rabbits of every possible description twitched their noses and hopped about, ears flopping. Some munched the new spring grass; others seemed happy to bask in the rising sun and sniff the air. Here and there, gangs of baby rabbits chased one another and played hide and seek, darting in and out of their burrows.

"Dad…what…how…?"

Her father smiled. Dorothee had never seen him look so young.

"I used to come here with my father when I was your age, but I forgot all about it until now. Every year about this time, all the rabbits come out of their burrows like this. I don't know why." They watched the rabbits in silence for a while longer. Then, taking off his glasses as he always did when he had something important to say, he said, "You mean the world to me, daughter. You just mean the world to me." And he bent down his head so that their foreheads were touching and whispered, "I don't know what I'd do without you."

He put his arm around her and they looked back out across the valley, where a new generation of bunnies lolloped happily in the tall green grass. Dorothee took a deep sip of hot chocolate from the warm thermos and snuggled up against her father's side. Spring had arrived, and hot chocolate had never tasted so good.

DISCUSSION QUESTIONS:

Dorothee's time with her father, watching the rabbits and having an early breakfast, brings up feelings of wonder. She feels lots of love for her dad and gratitude for the gifts of her life. Can you recall an experience like this—one that was so wonderful that you almost didn't have words to describe it?

The Perfect Party

KELLEN WAS ELEVEN THE summer she moved to
Rockford Springs with her family. They all really
liked living in Swedeport, their old town, but her mom got
a new job and so they had to move. Kellen missed her old
neighborhood and her school, but most of all, she missed
her friends.

It didn't take Kellen long to make up her mind about
Rockford Springs. It *stank*! It was a much smaller town
than Swedeport, and there was nothing to do. She hadn't
made any new friends yet, so Kellen spent most of her
free time moping around the house. She also spent a
lot of time down in the basement all by herself. Nobody

knew what she was doing down there, and she didn't want to talk about it. Her parents were worried about her.

When summer vacation was almost over, Kellen's mom had a terrific idea. While Kellen did whatever she usually did down in the basement, her mom picked up the phone and got to work. At lunch, Kellen was listlessly picking at her sandwich when she noticed a strange and disturbing look in her mother's eyes. *Uh-oh,* she thought. *This can't be good.*

"Honey, I had the best idea!" her mom sang. "You'll love it. I'm thinking that since this is the last weekend before school starts, and since I know you're worried about meeting all those new kids, I thought, 'Wouldn't it be better to start making friends *before* school starts?'"

Kellen just sat, waiting for the axe to fall.

"So I called up the school and got a list of all the kids in your new class and then I called their parents and invited all of them to a giant pool party bash *right here in our backyard*!"

For a moment, Kellen was speechless.

"Isn't that *great*?" her mom rambled on, oblivious to Kellen's mortified expression.

"No. It's not *great*. Mom! You can't do that. I am so

embarrassed! What do any of those kids care about me or my stupid pool?"

"I'm so surprised, honey. Just a couple years ago, you would have been really excited about this. I see you aren't, but it's too late now to cancel. Everyone's already been invited. People are coming…"

"Go ahead, have your party, but I won't come. I'll just stay in my room the whole time and I won't come out even for a *minute*!"

"I even hired a clown!" Mom said.

"*Mom!*"

"I'm kidding. Of course I didn't hire a clown. But honey, it really is too late to cancel the party. Unless you want to call everyone yourself and tell them not to come."

Kellen sat in sullen silence for a minute or so, and then said, "Fine. We'll have a party, but I am going to hate every minute of it."

This is going to be a disaster, she thought as she trudged back down to the basement.

And so, Saturday morning rolled around to find the back yard of Kellen's house festively decorated and filled with fifth graders. They clustered into small groups, none of which had any place for Kellen. Nobody put so much as a toe into the swimming pool, even though it was hot outside. To make matters worse, Kellen discovered that she had outgrown her swimsuit since last summer. It was way too tight.

The boys seemed content to gobble down all the food piled up on the long table next to the pool, but everyone else was just kind of standing around. Kellen knew she was supposed to do something, say something, but she didn't know what to do. Most of the kids didn't even realize it was her party—which was probably a good thing, since it had all the hallmarks of a total flop. After a while, though, some of the kids started swimming, and once that happened, the party wasn't a complete disaster. Still, Kellen had not worked up the courage to say much to anyone.

One minute, the sky was blue and cloudless. The next, it was filling with threatening clouds. The wind picked up and the air chilled. Kids started to get out of the pool. And then the sky started to turn all greenish. A hush fell over the yard and the birds went quiet. Everything was very still, and then, in the far distance, they heard a siren going off.

"Tornado!" someone yelled.

September is the beginning of tornado season in Wisconsin, and all the kids except Kellen knew exactly what to do. In the blink of an eye, they had gathered their

stuff and started toward the house. Kellen's mom came out and looked at the sky with a befuddled expression on her face. "What's going on?" she asked.

"They say a tornado's coming, Mom!" Kellen said, almost in tears. She'd never lived in tornado country before, and neither had her mom. Neither of them knew what to do.

"Where's your basement?" asked one kid from the party. "We need to go down into the basement until the warning is over."

"Oh, of course. Right. The basement. Come on, kids,

let's get moving!" Kellen's mom barked as the sky grew darker.

It wasn't a big basement. No video games, no carpeting, just a washer and dryer and piles of dirty laundry. As the kids packed into the basement, Kellen felt more embarrassed than ever, even after her mom brought down pillows and blankets to make the cement floor more comfortable. Before the power went out, her mom found a big box of candles, flashlights and camping lanterns, plus one transistor radio, among the few unpacked boxes against one wall. And so they sat and waited for the storm to blow through. Mom sat nearby trying to hear the weather report on the staticky radio. Nobody was happy.

"Hey, what's this?" one of the boys asked from a dark corner of the room.

"Yeah, this is cool!" said a girl who was looking over his shoulder.

Everyone looked over and saw that the boys had found a huge, old-fashioned steamer trunk. It was a beautiful old thing, big enough to hide four kids during a game of hide-and-seek, and it wasn't dusty like everything else down there.

"It's nothing. Leave it alone," Kellen blurted out. But it

was too late. The other kids had already opened the trunk, and when they saw what was inside, they gasped.

Packed into the trunk were tons of old-fashioned clothes. There were small boxes of necklaces and scarves and gowns. There were bowler hats and derbies and collars and cuffs made of cardboard. There were stacks of old letters and postcards from over a hundred years ago, tied with faded pink ribbon. And there were lots and lots of photos, the olden-days kind where nobody smiles and everything looks brown.

Before Kellen could do anything to stop them, everybody was laughing and running around and putting on all kinds of ridiculous outfits. Kellen didn't think this was any fun at all. They had found her secret world. In the dim basement, her face burned with embarrassment.

And then, just when it couldn't get any worse, one of the girls opened up some notebooks she found in the trunk. "Hey, these aren't old at all!" she exclaimed. "These are new. I have exactly the same glitter pen! What are these? Are they stories?"

"Hey! Stop it! Those are *mine*!" someone yelled. As everyone stopped in their tracks, Kellen realized that those words had actually burst out of her own mouth. Her voice continued to rush ahead, although she wanted nothing more than to slink away in silence. "This is an old trunk from my great grandma's attic," she went on, her voice shaky with emotion. "These are my private notebooks and they are full of stories I make up about the people who live in the trunk."

Someone tittered, but most everyone else listened silently. Kellen took a deep breath.

"Well, they don't really live in the trunk, but I imagine the people in the photographs who used to wear all these clothes and I make up stories about them."

Everyone kept looking at her.

"And if you think that's stupid…well…YOU are stupid. I never wanted to have this party in the first place!" She slammed the trunk lid down and sat on it with a thud, crossing her arms over her chest.

There was silence for a minute, and then Tara, the most popular girl at the party, said, "That's so *cool*!"

Others piped up in agreement. "Will you read us one of your stories?" Tara asked. Everyone started clamoring for a story.

Before long, Kellen was not only telling her stories; she was assigning parts and advising on costuming. Soon, the basement was full of kids dressed in old-timey clothes, carrying fancy walking sticks and acting like the people in those stories.

Long after the tornado threat had passed and the power had come back on, all the kids stayed down in the basement in their own imaginary world. Kellen's party quickly turned into the best party anyone could remember. Kellen's mom lit some more candles and brought down lemonade to drink out of tea cups and little sandwiches on trays.

No one even thought about leaving until the parents started to show up, and then, they went home reluctantly. Watching them leave, Kellen knew everything would be just fine.

DISCUSSION QUESTIONS:
Kellen feels out of place at her own party. Have you ever felt out of place? Have you ever helped someone else feel more welcome?

We Are Not Afraid

A LONG TIME AGO, way before you were born, maybe about the time your parents were little kids, there was a special school called the Highlander Folk School. Highlander was in Tennessee, in the South. The whole school was nothing more than a few buildings set up on a beautiful hill, surrounded by green forests and farm fields.

The people at Highlander believed that all people are equal, that all people should be allowed to go to school, and that the most important thing people need to learn is how to work together and love one another.

Back then, believe it or not, African-Americans and white people were not allowed to go to the same schools, eat in the same cafeterias, or even get married to one another if they fell in love. But Myles Horton, the man who started the school, believed that all of that was nonsense. He thought all kinds of people of all kinds of colors and from all kinds of backgrounds should be able to work, play and go to school together. A lot of famous people were students at Highlander, including Rosa Parks and Martin Luther King, Jr.

So, although it was against the law back then for African-Americans and white people to attend the same school, there were always people of all colors at Highlander, learning and playing and working together.

One of the things they liked to do most at Highlander was to make music together. At one time, a whole big choir of African-American kids visited from Atlanta, Georgia, and they stayed at Highlander.

One night all the kids were watching a movie in the main hall. The lights were out so everyone could see the movie better. All of a sudden, several big cars roared up to the school and a lot of men with guns got out and barged inside.

Nobody knew who the men were, but it was obvious they meant trouble. They were mad that African-American kids and white kids were going to the same school. As these

men stormed into the Highlander Folk School, somebody turned off the movie projector. The whole place went completely dark.

The men with guns quickly realized that they had made a big mistake. None of them had been inside the school, so none of them knew where the light switches were. And on top of that, they had forgotten to bring flashlights. So they roared and yelled at the kids to turn on the lights.

None of the kids moved a muscle. Then, in the darkness, the kids began to sing.

They sang a song called "We Shall Overcome," a very famous song often sung by people who believe that people of all colors can live together in harmony. The words go like this:

We shall overcome

We shall overcome

We shall overcome some day

Oh deep in my heart I do believe

We shall overcome some day…

There are more words, words about walking hand in hand, being free, and all being together, the whole wide world around. In that scariest of all situations, those kids made up their own words, too. To the men with guns they sang:

We are not afraid

We are not afraid

We are not afraid today

Deep in my heart I still believe we are not afraid today

This really startled those gun-toting men.

The kids were supposed to be the scared ones, but now the grownups with weapons were starting to feel a little nervous. After some more fumbling around, they just gave up, ran back to their cars and drove away.

Those kids learned something important that night.

They learned how strong and brave they could be if they stuck together. And the words they made up that night have been a permanent part of the song ever since.

DISCUSSION QUESTIONS:
When the children sang about how they would overcome, what were they talking about? What did they want to overcome? Why were the children not afraid?

Acknowledgements

L IKE ANYTHING WORTH ANYTHING in life, *After Aesop* is the work of many hearts and hands, a product of community. This book would still be an idea if not for the vision, tirelessness and editorial wonderworking of the incomparable Melissa Block. Deep gratitude and admiration for illustrator Lisa Hedicker and her uncanny ability to see and to paint what has previously only existed in my mind's eye. Who would have thought I could collaborate so richly with an artist on the other side of the world?

Thanks also to Alex Abatie for designing this book and to Bob Fulmer, Geoff Connor Newlan and Linda Liker for their distinctly unglamorous but critical contributions. Special thanks to my wife Eliza, who is often my first reader, listener and gentle critic. Thanks for finding me when I get lost.

Last but not least, I want to thank the children of all ages who make up the Unitarian Society of Santa Barbara. The stories in this book do not arise from me alone, but from the thick web of life we weave together, week after week, year after year.

About the Author

Kim Fisher

The Rev. Aaron McEmrys serves as Senior Minister of the Unitarian Society of Santa Barbara. Aaron's past lives include work in the theatre, as a labor and community organizer and as the owner of a neighborhood game store, all of which provide rich fodder for the themes of creativity, justice and kindness that run through his stories. Aaron shares his life with his wife, Eliza, 4 kids, 2 cats and one golden retriever.

About the Illustrator

Lisa Hedicker is a children's illustrator from the UK. She works primarily in watercolors combining traditional painting with a love of the odd to create quirky characters and vibrant images.